LUCIFER'S DAUGHTER

PRINCESS OF HELL #1

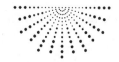

EVE LANGLAIS

1st Edition © August 2010, Eve Langlais

2nd Edition © November 2015, Eve Langlais

Cover Art by Amanda Kelsey RazzDazz Design © September 2015

Edited by Devin Govaere, Amanda L. Pederick

Produced in Canada

Published by Eve Langlais

http://www.EveLanglais.com

eBook ISBN: 978 1927 459 82 9

Ingram ISBN: 978-1-77384-011-6

CHAPTER ONE

Satan appeared in a puff of smoke that contained an acrid hint of brimstone. I glanced at him briefly, noticed his glower, and continued to paint my toenails a gorgeous seashell pink.

"You're a disgrace to your lineage." The Devil immediately started in on his favorite rant as he paced the small confines of my living room on the mortal plane.

"Yeah, yeah, I know," I said with disinterest, blowing on the wet coat of polish. "Whatever happened to hello? How are you doing?"

"That would require manners, something you know I abhor," he retorted.

"Well, could you at least try and knock before just appearing next time? I'm kind of fond of my

1

privacy, not to mention, as a girl, I could have been doing something–" I paused here, trying to think of something appropriate. Of course, I couldn't at the moment, but I would about an hour later when the conversation was long done. "Important. Or what if I was entertaining a gentleman caller?"

"You have a guy over?" The snort was because he knew me so well. "I wish I could catch you with a guy. Or even a girl. Why can't you be more like your half-sisters?" he railed.

"Um, probably because they're succubi and I'm part human."

"Minor details. Couldn't you at least sin a little? You're supposed to be a princess of Hell."

"I bet other princesses are lucky enough to have their dads knock first."

"See what I mean?" he said as he tossed his hands in exasperation. "No respect, which would usually make me proud, but you're not following through with vile acts. You're making me look like a bad parent. My minions in Hell are mocking me. There have even been rumors I'm no longer fit to be the Father of All Sin since I can't even control my own daughter."

"Whatever happened to being rewarded for

rebellions against our parents? I thought that was a huge sin."

"Rebelling with kind acts and the truth wasn't what I had in mind!"

"Yeah, well, it sucks to be you." I'd always been the good apple in a sea of bad ones, a fact that drove my dad—The Devil, Beelzebub, whatever you wanted to call him—wild.

"It wasn't bad enough you got straight As in school. Oh, no." He paced faster as he warmed up for his rant. "You just have to be a virgin, too. You're twenty-three years old. It's just wrong!" he shouted. "I raised you to be more evil than this."

He had. When people claimed their parents were cruel to them growing up and traumatized them for life, I laughed. I had them all beat. How many kids did you know who got rewarded for lying about staying up late at night reading—then got punished for doing something academic.

Standing, my pretty pink toenails glistening, I bristled, hands on my hips, as my dad and I faced off, once again over my lack of a sex life. A conversation that was disturbing in and of itself. "I told you before I am waiting for love. And if you don't like it, too bad!"

I wanted my first time to be special. Dad knew that and totally didn't respect it, which I expected. But in this, I would have my way.

I'd read enough books about sex to know this momentous occasion would be a memory that would last a lifetime, which, in my case, could be quite a while, given my parentage.

"You're being too bloody picky."

Maybe, but it wasn't entirely my fault I hadn't yet found *the one*. "Picky? Have you even stopped to consider the criteria this poor fellow has to meet?" I held up a finger. "One, he can't be completely mortal. You know I'm stronger than a normal human girl. What if I accidentally hurt him, you know, in the heat of the moment?"

"A little pain can go a long way in the boudoir." The Devil winked.

I grimaced. "Ew. So gross. Now I'm going to have to bleach my mind."

A scowl creased his features. "You are such a prude. I blame my brother for that."

"Uncle God has nothing to do with my disinterest in your sex life." Growing up, all I ever heard about was how my father was desired by women worldwide. Ugh. Nothing worse than knowing the demon girls who had me over for playdates had single moms looking to hook up with my father.

"I don't know how, but I'll bet he's somehow to blame for your stance on this whole abstinence thing. Sex is a natural act."

"Natural?" My turn to snort. "You wouldn't know natural if it smacked you in the face."

"I'll have you know I do so know the difference between natural boobs slapping me and fake ones. It's all in the squeeze factor."

I groaned. "Again, too much info. And part of the reason why I'm having such a hard time finding the right guy. How many men do you know who won't run screaming when they find out my dad happens to be Satan, master of lies and deceit?"

"That is a good point. They should be scared. Debauching my daughter! I won't stand for it."

"You are so difficult."

"I know. It's one of my most endearing traits."

Actually, it was. With my dad you never knew what to expect. He had his own sense of morals—and style. But his wardrobe choices were a topic for another time. "If you're fishing for compliments, then go elsewhere. I am not going to cater to your already immense ego."

"Me, conceited?" He smiled. "Why thank you.

That's the nicest thing anyone has said to me all day."

Arrogance, a sin my father lived by, which was akin to shallowness, which I'm afraid I had to admit I kind of suffered to. In my case, I was shallow enough to want a guy who was hot, hot enough to melt my insides into mushy goo and make me cross-eyed with desire.

Those were just the top three criteria for my as-yet-unknown fantasy lover; I had a few more, but I had yet to meet someone who managed to get past all three, which made me wonder if I needed to revise my list.

But do I really want to compromise? Not really. I knew I'd find the one eventually, but while I waited for Mister Right, I had to say, I quite enjoyed driving my dad batty.

A frustrated devil pulled at his still-dark hair, which held only hints of grey at the temples, and sighed wearily. "Why do you do this to me?" He slumped onto the couch, expression woebegone. "I only want what's best for me and my reputation. Is that too much to ask for?"

Poor Daddy. I sat down beside him and hugged his stocky body. After all, when all was said and done, I loved my father, even if he could be a tad overbearing and a bad influence.

In an effort to cheer him up, I said, "Hey, if it's any consolation, once I do find the guy, I probably won't wait to get married first. That's a little sin, right?"

"I guess."

Of course, my decision to skip marriage might have to do with the fact that I couldn't enter a church without all the religious items bursting into flame. So unfair. I hadn't done anything evil—well, truly evil—and yet God and all his trappings reacted to me as if I was the anti-Christ, something my half-brother found highly amusing.

Even priests couldn't get close to me; well, the pure ones, anyway. The bad ones had no problem at all. It was only the pure of faith following the doctrine of the One God who dropped to the floor writhing in agony. Good thing most of the priests I met were of the other variety.

Needless to say, I didn't think marriage lay in the cards unless I did the whole city-hall-judge thing, which I personally thought lacked romance and commitment.

Despite my attempt to mollify him, my dad still

sat on the couch, looking as if I'd graduated with honors all over again. Good thing none of his minions were around to see. It was probably some kind of sin that a part of me was glad to know that, around me, Daddy didn't feel as if he had to put on an act. I mean, it had to be hard, being evil all the time. Even bad guys needed a break—and someone to love them.

"Dad, I know what will cheer you up. Why don't you go back to Hell and torture a few of the demons who are bad-mouthing you and show them you're still boss? Start a few eternal fires, make a grand speech about everyone bowing to the king of Hades or facing the flames of perdition."

"You're just trying to get rid of me," he said, his tone sulky. Although I could see my words had perked him up a bit.

"Yes and no. I have to open the bar in, like, twenty minutes; so, yes, I am trying to get you to leave, but," I said, throwing my arms around him and hugging him tight, "I love you, and I don't like to see you like this."

"I don't know why, but I'm attached to you, too. Probably some kind of mental defect," Satan said grumpily as he hugged me back. Despite his conviction that affection meant some kind of disease, I cherished moments like these; they tended to be few and far between. "Try to be bad," were his last words before popping out of sight.

The smell of brimstone—the predominant perfume of Hell, and my dad's calling card—hung in the air, the hard-to-wash miasma clinging to my sweater. Great, now I needed to change again. I was on this plane incognito. As in, trying to live a some-what normal life.

Hurrying, because I was now definitely running late, I changed my yellow crew-neck T-shirt to a tight, pink, scoop-necked one. I tucked it into my skin-tight white jeans, and then I yanked on my pink ankle boots with furry cuffs because everyone knew, no matter how fabulous the clothes, it was all about the footwear. I grabbed my keys and white lambs-wool jacket and hightailed it out the door.

As soon as I exited the building, the wind caught at my hair. Stupid me, I'd left the almost waist-length locks loose. The long, silken strands plastered them-selves across my face and restricted my view. Through the hairy skein, I could see only in patches.

With no time to go back and tie it up, I squinted as best as I could and cursed—some of it pretty color-ful, considering the people I knew—and trudged off to work.

However, the gods were conspiring against me.

And by gods, I specifically meant Loki, that Norse deity of mischief. Turn the god of tricks down for a date, and ever since, gusts of wind arose out of nowhere plastering my hair to my face and brick walls suddenly appeared.

And I walked face first into it.

Oomph.

CHAPTER TWO

Okay, so it wasn't a brick wall but a man, a very solidly built man. A man I'd hit quite hard.

Of course, I didn't intend to take the blame. "Ow, watch where you're standing." In other words, how dare he get in my way? When would the denizens of the mortal plane realize the world revolved around me? Not conceit. Daddy said so.

The problem with hitting immovable objects—and this guy was built like a brick house—was the bounce factor. That would be me.

Rebounding from him, I stumbled backwards, and I might have regained my balance had my left heel not caught on the lip of the curb. Damn my adorable footwear for trying to bring me down.

Arms out to my sides, flapping uselessly, I teetered over the edge, and I would have probably fallen on my ass in the street had the rock I'd run into not grabbed me by the arms. He held me steady but offered no apology.

"You should watch where you're walking," said a gravelly voice that made goose bumps rise on every part of my body.

"I didn't see you." The truth. How it would make my father sob.

"No shit, Cousin Itt." Had he just compared me to a certain hairball? "You might want to invest in some hair elastics."

No kidding. Insults aside—which really didn't bother me given I could lob my fair share—I really wanted to see his face, to see if he could possibly be as sexy as his voice suggested, but the damned hair wound around my face just refused to get out of the way.

I'm beginning to understand the appeal of a pixie cut. Now if only I wasn't so vain about my silken threads. *See, Daddy, I'm not perfect.*

Since he held my arms still, I couldn't sweep the strands from my face and only managed an impression of height and width. Steady on my feet once again, he released me, but by the time I'd managed to grab my hair and yank it to the side, the stranger had disappeared.

Hunh. Where did he go?

I looked ahead of me, behind me, and even across the street; but the humans stumbling along didn't seem right. For one, they seemed too ordinary.

The man I'd bumped into had felt like something *more*. Who could fail to notice the power coiled inside him, an energy my own senses reacted to?

He felt...delicious. And he must have been new in town because I could state with certainty that I'd never met him before; and not to sound conceited, but anyone with supernatural abilities—be they good or evil—ended up in my bar at some point. Speaking of which, I was late!

Walking quickly, I made the remaining six blocks in under fifteen minutes, arriving just as Charon popped out of a dimensional door inside the alcove that hid the entrance to my place. Lucky guy had the permission and power to open a rift between the mortal plane and Hell.

Princess or not, I had to rely on either dear old dad or public interdimensional transportation. The shame of it—and the smell.

"Don't you have to ferry souls across the river?" I asked my most faithful client in what was a long-standing joke between us.

"I'm thirsty," he said, his face hidden in the

depths of the voluminous cloak he always wore. "Besides, they're dead. They can wait. After all, they have all of eternity left." Charon chuckled, a chilly sound to those who didn't know him.

"Oh, give it up," I said. I punched him in the arm, er, the sleeve before unlocking the door to the bar. "You and I both know you're about as evil as a fly."

"I've known some pretty evil flies in my time," he said, dead pan. Then he chuckled, losing the staid tone. "Actually, I took the night off. My wife says I need to slow down, so I've got my son working the boat today. Here's to hoping Adexios doesn't drop the oar this time and strand the souls in the middle of the Styx again."

"He didn't?" I breathed, unable to hide my shock. Talk about a major faux pas.

"I'm afraid he did," said Charon, shaking his head. "I love my son, but I have to say, he's not the sharpest scythe in the armory. I acted pre-emptively this time though; I tethered the oar to the boat."

I laughed, and let my longtime friend—who also happened to be Dad's best friend—into the bar. He kept me company while I fired on the lights and prepped the bar for the evening crowd. Thursday nights usually got quite the crowd, but with *Survivor:*

Burn in Hell premiering that night on the Damned Channel, I knew we'd be missing a few familiar faces. Heck, I was taping it at home on my DVR. I never missed a season or an episode.

Its premiere reminded me of how much I really needed to invest in a flat screen; another thing on my lengthy to-do list for when I made some money. I refused to borrow money from Dad because he always tried to tie it up in strings and clauses with sub-clauses. I intended to keep my soul—if I had one —thank you very much.

The bar, that I'd named Nexus, was mine, lock, stock, and mortgage. My retro-eighties tavern— because that was the only era where rock truly counted—served as a haven for all the abnormal people in the area. And by abnormal, I didn't mean the escaped mental institution kind, but more the hey-I-hear-voices-because-I-see-ghosts and staff-wielding, long-bearded kind.

I should add that my bar becoming a gathering spot for special folk living up top was not my idea. Originally, I'd just wanted a regular karaoke bar, with salted peanuts and pricy cocktails, but of course, bad blood will always interfere. In my case, my satanic side mixed with who-knows-what.

Whatever had created me, other than dear old

Lucifer, had packed a potent punch. With no effort on my part, the space around me for about a dozen feet or so ended up being a magic-free zone. Seriously, I was like a walking null field. That didn't stop the natural-born abilities of the supernaturals who liked to frequent my place, but it sure came in handy when humans with their own brand of magic started lobbing fireballs or zapping with lightning. It was the price one paid when too many people with magic gathered and drank.

Falling-down-drunken warlocks arguing over who possessed the most powerful grimoire? Never good. Unless you were in Nexus, of course; then all you saw were two old men swinging feeble punches, instead of devastating earthquakes, and meteors falling from the sky. Once word got around about my mostly magic-free bar, it became the hottest place in town for supernatural beings to hang out, and yet the mortals just walked on by. Funny coincidence, that, or was that the hand of my Aunt Karma?

She always did say I was her favorite demonic niece.

At least my special patrons tipped well—if they didn't want spit in their drink. Don't judge. My staff worked hard, and they deserved proper compensation.

The fact that I made sure they were treated right made it easy to find staff. I had several dryads who acted as barmaids, their willowy figures and swaying limbs able to gracefully sway through even the thickest crowd. Then there was Percy, my bartender and bouncer, who, with his half-giant blood, tended to get very little lip, a fact he lamented on more than one occasion.

"How am I supposed to get any exercise?" he rumbled. Apparently, Gerry the rat shifter's comment to try living under a bridge was just the excuse Percy needed to go for a run.

I'd have to make sure to credit a few beers on Gerry's tab for helping me out with employee satisfaction.

To round out my happy working family, there was little ol' me. Okay, maybe not so little at about five foot nine, over six in heels, and packing a nice left hook.

On the nights Percy was off, to save my manicure, I made sure to keep my handy-dandy baseball bat within close reach behind the bar—because swords were totally frowned upon in the mortal world—and if people got out of hand, bam, right in the kisser.

During my teen years, I'd played baseball in the

demon female league and developed a wicked swing. But even without my bat, I wasn't completely helpless.

Like hello, I was the daughter of the devil. Of course, no one at the bar, except for Charon and Percy, knew I was related to the big guy himself. For one, I didn't want any favoritism. A girl got seriously tired of people using her only to curtail favor with her dad.

But that wasn't the only reason I didn't announced my parentage. For some reason, strangers seemed to think trying to kidnap a princess of Hell gave them leverage over my dad. Wow, were they wrong, and yet no matter how many times I showed them the error of their ways—sometimes in a kind of violent and deadly fashion—they just didn't get it. The attacks by those who figured out my guise kept coming, or least those attacks had happened often when I lived in Hell.

Up here, on the mortal plane, out of the HBC news eye, and banning Daddy from visiting me at work, I was more or less able to live incognito. Instead of going by my first name, Satana, I used my middle name, Muriel. As to my special powers, the patrons assumed I was some kind of a witch and left me alone.

It's kind of refreshing, actually, to be considered normal.

When I'd lived in Hell, I'd constantly had to prove myself—not to mention save my own life. With flashing eyes—in which some claimed they could see the fires of Hell—I put those who would cross me or try to hurt my daddy back in line. Thankfully, that didn't happen often anymore. My reputation—not to mention my lineage—tended to precede me when I returned to visit.

Stupid Hump Day family dinners. My father knew I found them torturous, hence why he kept having them.

My full name, by the way, for those who really got stuck on the niceties—and wanted to piss off my dad—was Satana Muriel Baphomet. Bastard daughter of Satan, born of an unknown mother whom we never talked about, mostly because even the thought of her gave me a vicious migraine. Given that I practically hit the ground convulsing thinking about her, and dad never saw fit to explain why, we kind of ignored the subject, the whole ignorance was bliss quite true in my world.

At five foot nine, and lushly rounded, I could admit I was definitely not a size 6, but ask me if I cared. I preferred my lush frame to the starved look of today's models. People meeting me for the first time tended to admire my black hair that reached almost to my ass, streaked with reddish highlights, all natural, which still freaked my hairdresser out. Boring brown eyes except when I channeled my inner fury, and then they shone with flames, just like my daddy. And because I had no shame, I could admit I possessed lips made for sucking cock—or so I'd been told. I'd yet to test that theory. Say hello to the most surprising twenty-three-year-old virgin. Hopefully not for much longer. I intended to pop that cherry as soon as I fell in love. Not just lust, love.

Speaking of lust, look what just walked in. Three hot and sexy hunks. A come-fuck-me vibe practically oozed from their skin. Seriously, if I could have bottled these guys, I would have made a fortune even greater than the creator of Viagra did. Every red-blooded, and one cold-blooded, female in the bar eyeballed them as they licked their lips. Even the males in the place stopped to take notice.

It could have been the fact that they had an aura about them that said, "I am the badass your daddy would go to jail for killing." In other words, totally the type of guy my dad would love. The type of guy I usually avoided because I couldn't stand arrogant, conceited and... Fuck, I was lying. I totally loved a guy with swagger.

I was such a good daughter, and this good daughter was totally digging these fellows. It could have been the fact that I coveted the leather, ankle-length duster one of them wore. *Strip that coat off, sweetcheeks.* And not just so I could steal it, I wanted a peek at what hid under it.

Whatever super pheromone they radiated, it also helped that all three of them were fucking gorgeous. Wet panty alert. Someone crank up the air conditioning.

Resisting the urge to fan myself, I instead frowned. I could practically smell the hand of my father here. I mean, come on. What were the chances that, on the same day Daddy Dear showed up whining about my virgin state, these three most perfect hunks of male flesh walked into my bar?

Trust dear old Dad to pull out the big guns, and judging by the bulges these guys packed in their tight jeans, big might prove an understatement. And, surprise, they just happened to be my three favorite flavors!

Ranging from six foot one-ish to about six foot six, they were like a rainbow of boy candy—blond, brunette, and ebony. Broad shoulders stretched their jackets while their faces presented chiseled perfection. Even yummier, they moved with a smooth grace, nothing awkward or hesitant about them. I loved a man with confidence, and now I had three to ogle.

An ogle that narrowed down to one when the ebony-haired one suddenly glanced my way. Upon spotting me, the aloofness in his bearing dissipated. Shoulders went back even further, the spine straightened and his gaze narrowed, focusing in on me. Without ever angling his head, he checked me out, undressed me with his eyes.

My poor panties didn't stand a chance, and if I hadn't been the only bartender currently working, I might have skipped off to my office and masturbated.

Don't judge. A virgin to sex didn't mean I was completely innocent or without some needs. I'd long ago learned how to please myself, and that helped me fight the temptations of the flesh.

An inability to deal with this particular temptation, though, put me in a foul mood. I really hated not being in control. Cross that a stranger could affect me so, I turned my back on them as they strolled leisurely to the bar. Ignoring them visually didn't mean I resisted taking a sniff. I inhaled the intoxicating scent of men's cologne, soap, and that musk everyone emitted that was almost as distinctive as a fingerprint.

Damn they smell good. Delicious even. I wonder how they taste.

"Can I get a beer?" The deep baritone caressed my skin, and I couldn't help but shiver. That kind of voice could prove so dangerous.

It made a girl want to do things...

Naughty things.

I restrained myself—barely. All it took was reminding myself these guys were probably bait.

You aren't going to win, Daddy. I had more willpower than to fall for some hunky eye candy. I clung tight to my morals, which didn't take a big hand, given how few I had.

Given my decision to pretend the hotties behind me didn't exist, I polished the glass in my hand more vigorously than required.

"I don't think she likes you. Probably because you forgot the magic word," teased a more mellow voice behind me, its smooth honey texture just as yummy. "Pay attention and feel free to take notes. This is how we talk to a gorgeous woman. I'm sorry, beautiful. I don't blame you for ignoring my rude friend over here. Let me assure you that, while he might not know his manners, I do. I have no problem saying please. And later, if you're free, I'd like to thank you in person."

My eyebrows lifted, and I really had to struggle not to laugh. Did that line seriously ever work? Although I had to say, his blatant interest did pique my vain side. I sucked in my stomach and stuck my chest out a bit farther. So sue me—no, really, try. My dad had great lawyers, and I could use the money— for falling under his complimentary spell. A girl could only resist so much.

"Oh, for fuck's sake," uttered a gravelly voice with a hint of disgust. "Would you stop tiptoeing around? It's a bar. She works here. Wench, get us some beers, would you, or do you need more time to get over yourself?"

Upon hearing his voice, I froze with my back still turned. Could it be? Had fate brought back the stranger from earlier?

I thought Aunt Fate was still on vacation. Something about she deserved some time off and people could make their own damned beds and lie in them while she got a tan.

Intrigued by the guy's complete lack of manners —which my dad would have totally cheered—and determined to finally see what he looked like, I turned around, only to realize I had no idea who the uncouth voice belonged to. All three of them eyed me.

Grabbing a clear glass stein, I pressed on the tap and filled it with some ale. Forget asking them what type. They'd drink what I served them.

First mug filled, I slapped it in front of the blond, who opened his eyes wide. So cute, with a hint of innocence.

I could totally corrupt him.

Except his low baritone as he uttered, "Thank you," told me he wasn't the one I wanted. Although perhaps I shouldn't be too hasty. He had the chiseled face of an underwear model and the blond hair of a surfer.

As my slutty sister Bambi would say, "I wouldn't kick him out of bed."

But he wasn't the one I was curious about. A second mug of beer, bearing a foamy froth, set in front of the brown-haired fellow. His slow smile let me know I had found the want-to-be Lothario even before he spoke. "Thank you, sexy."

I ignored him, not as easy as it sounded. With his bright blue eyes and engaging smile, he surely got into more than his fair share of panties.

A man whore, though, wasn't what I aspired to.

And besides, I now had, through the process of elimination, found my man.

As I filled a third mug, I peeked at Mister Gravelly Voice, the same guy I'd rammed into on my way to work.

That expression, breath caught? Oh yeah. Totally applied once I looked upon his face. I couldn't help but stare, utterly intrigued by the man —and caught in the grips of some severe lust because, damn, he was so my type.

Unruly ebony hair, an angular face, a wicked scar that went across his cheek, and the most piercing green eyes I'd ever seen. His lips twisted in a bit of a smirk at my perusal.

"Take a picture. It will last longer."

"I would, but I forgot my phone at home." I lied. Daddy would be so proud. Especially given I continued to rudely stare. I couldn't help myself, but he didn't like it.

"Get a good enough look yet? Are you one of those chicks who digs scars?" His lip turned into an even more impressive sneer. "I've got an even better one to show you if you want to go somewhere a little more private."

Ooh, attitude. I liked that in a man, just ask my nipples since they seemed determined to drill through my shirt to say hello. "Who cares about your scar?" I said with a sweet smile. Having learned from the best sluts Hell had to offer, I leaned forward so that the shadow formed by my cleavage distracted him. He was a man; he couldn't resist. My grin widened. "I have scars, too, baby, some that make yours look like a shaving cut." At least until I got some more of that cream Nefertiti made. My dad's sorceress was a veritable fount of magical beauty products, if you could pay the price. "Just so you know, I wasn't staring at your battle marks. I was more interested in your coat. Where'd you get it?"

I truly wanted to know, even as I lied about checking him out.

"Why would a girl like you have scars? Cut yourself shaving?"

"More like slicing and dicing," and making demonic julienne flesh fries. It should be noted that those who dared mark me no longer posed a threat. I didn't believe in leaving loose ends, or enemies.

I think I caught Green-eyes by surprise; I could see I'd shocked his friends. They started laughing. I turned a disdainful, ice-princess look on them, one that gruff-voice aped; and under our dual stares, the two shut up pretty quickly—which made them go down a notch in my esteem. Real men would not be cowed by a dirty look.

"I think we'll get a table," muttered the blond. Grabbing his beer, he and his friend-of-the-flowery-speeches scooted across the room to a booth tucked against the back wall. Actually, all my tables hugged a wall; funny, how paranoid supernatural beings could be. It made for an odd setup, but a great dance floor. The elves especially liked all the space for dancing when they'd had a few too many nectars.

Gravelly-voice watched his friends leave then turned back to face me. "Who are you?" he asked.

"The bartender." Smart-ass comments were my specialty.

"Seriously. Who are you?" he asked again, looking at me intently with his green eyes, whose brightness and clarity reminded me of soft spring grass. They contrasted nicely with his dark-and-dangerous look.

"Who are you?" I flashed back.

"I'm Auric."

Auric, now there was a name you didn't hear every day. I liked it, though. It felt *masculine*. "I'm Muriel, the bartender." I gave him my middle name and skipped my first and last, for obvious reasons.

"No," he said, the word emerging slowly, his expression thoughtful. "You're more than that."

Perceptive of him. "Aren't we all more than we appear?" I gestured to my usual mixed crowd of elves, dryads, gnomes, and other beings thought to belong in fairy tales. Oh, and there was even a demon in the back. He'd gotten thrown out of Hell for being too soft on the suffering and was now currently drowning his sorrows with a couple of martinis—stirred, with two olives. Pussy.

"Maybe I should ask what you are. You've got a strange flavor to you." With his attention focused on me, I could inhale, not just with my nose, but my senses to his aura. An aura unlike any I'd tasted before. His own brand of uniqueness radiated from him—not quite good, yet not evil. How fascinating. Whatever he oozed, it started a chain reaction in my body. My nipples hardened, and I licked my lips, a sensual motion that caught his attention; and, for a moment, I saw his eyes flash. It would seem Auric was not immune to my charms.

"You can feel my power?" he asked, his brows pulling together in a crease.

Oops. I might have divulged a little too much. Time to divert his suspicions. I smiled and shrugged. "I can do a lot of things, just like everyone else in here. From what I sensed of your friends, they're special, too." The blond had a bestial smell to him, signaling shape shifter, while Blue-eyes had the ozone feel of a wizard. An interesting trio, to be sure.

"They're special, all right," Auric muttered.

"You guys must be new. I don't think I've ever seen you around before."

"We moved to town a few months ago, but have been traveling on...*business*." His hesitation caught my attention.

"Oh, what kind of business are you into?"

"This and that," was his vague reply.

"How did this and that bring you to the bar?"

"We happened to hear about the bar from a client. He said the owner is a unique kind of supernatural. No one seems to know exactly who or what she is. We thought we'd check it out."

"Aah, the boss," I said, hiding a smile. "Yes, she's something, all right." I wondered just what outrageous stories he'd heard about me. Good ones I hoped. A girl did like to know she was making a reputation for herself.

"Does she ever come in?" he questioned.

Why all the interest in the bar owner, in other words me? Unease coiled in my stomach, as if I needed that to know I should guard my words. "The boss rarely comes in. She just lets us peons do the work for her."

"What a shame; I would have liked to meet her. But I have to ask, if she's not around, how does the no-magic thing work?"

Shit. He knew about that. Then again, who didn't?

"No idea how it works." I shrugged.

"Are you sure she's not here?"

"What makes you think she might be?"

"Because it feels as if the whole joint has, like, a dampening field on it. I would have thought she'd have to be present for it to work, or is it more like a spell?"

Enough was enough. This barrage of questions was really starting to irk. This talkative Auric didn't seem like the guy who'd walked into the bar, or who I'd bumped into today. That guy had attitude; that guy didn't beat around the bush. So why the seemingly innocent questions and friendly talk? A man like him should be demanding answers—pinning me against a wall, his face in my space, close enough for him to threaten, and kiss.

Something didn't seem right, and not just my continued lust for him. This stranger should have been asking questions about me—hot bartender with an awesome set—not who owned the bar and how it worked. For the confused, even if he was inadvertently talking about me, I didn't like it. I'd been the victim of too many assassination attempts not to feel my hackles go up in warning.

Enough was enough. I switched on a tactic that had worked well for me in the past. "Yeah the no-magic thing is totally neat," I said, adopting my ditsiest routine—my succubus sister Bambi taught me well. Airhead in Motion; drama 101 at the School of Hard Knocks that Bambi taught as a professor—not because she wanted to. The terms of her parole forced her.

Who knew that judge would have a fit her husband slept with a succubus?

I batted my lashes for good measure. Oh and wetted my lips as I opened my eyes wide and said, "The whole like no-magic thing is like so totally cool." The only way I could have made that moment even more TSTL—for those who suddenly feel a need to Google search, it stands for too stupid to live —would have been to snap a piece of gum. Sugar free, of course, because I wasn't going back to my dad's dentist, the tooth sadist. Dare to show up with too much plaque and you were in trouble.

I not only brushed but flossed regularly now. *You should too. You've been warned.*

An impromptu cough covered my urge to evil cackle. I couldn't let Auric know I was screwing with him—mentally, not physically, unfortunately.

Good news. My bubbly response threw him for a loop. His eyes narrowed in consideration.

Oops, maybe I'd laid it on a little thick, the problem with a dramatic father, a flair for the over-the-top.

"There's something different about you, Muriel," mused Auric.

Gee, do you think? Smirk. I was almost tempted to ask him what he sensed about me, but one, that smacked of too much interest. Playing hard to get was the way to go with a guy like him.

Taught during Snag That Bad Boy, the advanced class 304. Good thing my sister was sleeping with that teacher or I might have flunked.

Apparently, I was a little too alpha—which sounded totally muscle bound and not feminine at all—to totally cow to what a bad boy wanted in a woman.

"Why can't a bad girl get a bad boy?" I'd asked.

The whole class answered, "Because Ms. XXX

said so," it not being the first time I'd wondered aloud.

Pompous bitch. I totally took my sister out for lunch the day she dumped the teacher. The day after I got my grades and passed of course.

Back to Auric though. And my interest in him. More the point his lack of interest in me.

Like hello, talking to me for at least five minutes now and he'd yet to ask me out.

What kind of guy made an effort to pump me for information instead of humping me in the buff? Not that I would agree, but still, I expected an attempt to be made.

My irrational irritation and the reason behind it made me decide the time had come to end this conversation. Quickly too, before I slipped up and said something that revealed who and what I was.

But he spoke first, "What do you say we go somewhere quieter after you finish your shift? Somewhere we could *talk*?" Nice try with the innuendo.

Too little too late for my rather offended ego. Especially since I was sure his talk wouldn't involve his tongue and my tongue hanging out. "Sorry. I'm busy tonight." With that, I turned my back on him. But I really didn't like doing it.

It wasn't that I feared him coming over the bar,

knife in hand, ready to impale me. More that I didn't want to turn away from him. A part of me wanted to keep talking and staring and...dragging him over the granite top and sucking on that lower lip.

Sigh. And that insane reaction was why I needed to put some distance between us. For a moment he sat there. I know he did because I felt the weight of his stare between my shoulder blades.

Not a word. Not a touch. Not even a quiver of sound, and yet, for some reason I could swear I knew he was amused by my reaction. Amused and surprised.

Good.

I hated being predictable.

The moment he left the bar to join his friends, and I knew because a part of me tried to trail after, a smidgen of disappointment hit me. But why?

Good grief. It seemed a stupid, girly part of me really wanted him to try harder. *Why didn't he try harder?*

Had I lost my sexual edge? Had my virgin status finally started sapping my seductive wiles?

A dwarf sat down at the bar, his long red beard held in a twisted tail from his chin, the metal bands binding it intricately carved. A warrior then. One battle scarred, ooh, and married. A true challenge to test myself and make sure everything was in working order.

Adjusting my beauties and wetting my lips, I sashayed to the hydrant-shaped male with his massive beaked nose that required size to offset his bushy brows.

Elbows hitting the bar first, I leaned forward—*do your jobs, ladies*—and let my cleavage talk to the male who thought short, hairy women were the sexiest thing since the invention of hand cream.

"Hey." *Look at the boobs. My magical boobs.* "What are you drinking?" A little jiggle and...

Bam. His eyes glazed over, and he said, "Urg."

The skunky dark ale I slapped in front of him sloshed over the rim. I held out my hand, and the dwarf slid me a twenty, which I tucked in my bra while he watched. His eyes rolled up, and he fell off his stool.

I peeked over. No blood. Dwarves had hard heads. He'd be fine in a minute, and meanwhile, I had my answer.

This body is in bangin' form tonight. So something had to be wrong with Auric.

Maybe he had a steady girlfriend? That could be fixed.

Goodness but I was just full of evil today. My

dad and my situation must have gotten to me a lot more than I knew. Knowing I was off balance, it seemed prudent—and, yes, petty—to ignore Auric and his friends the rest of the evening. Sticking to my spot behind the bar, I let my dryad barmaids on duty serve them.

Did a teensy tiny part of me hope that Auric would perhaps find his way back?

A tiny part, which I kept mentally stomping, especially since it didn't happen.

Auric didn't leave the booth he was in, and neither did his friends. Although I caught him watching me speculatively more than once. Not that I checked on him. Nope, not me. I just happened to be keeping a general eye on the joint.

The fact that I watched his corner closest meant I'd pegged him for the biggest threat in the place.

But he did nothing.

What a jerk.

When three a.m. hit, I flashed the lights to signal closing time.

The drunken, disgraced demon, who now sang Elton John, staggered out the door. Which left only three patrons in the bar.

"Time to go, boys," I announced and then proceeded to ignore them as I wiped the bar.

Appearing nonchalant didn't mean I felt it. If those guys were planning anything, it would happen now, when I was alone, Percy having left at my insistence. The day I couldn't handle a couple of guys, was the day my Bitch of Hell card would get revoked.

The three of them exited the booth and began walking across the floor. The steady thumps of their footsteps let me gauge their location without appearing to pay them any mind.

Thump. Thump. Thump.

Close and closer, then walking past me. Unbidden, my gaze lifted from the gleaming granite in time to see Auric striding by, his gaze trained on me, enigmatic, and yet...something flashed between us.

In another breath, they were gone.

From the back, Silvia, my wood nymph waitress, emerged, wrapping a gossamer scarf around her neck.

"I'll see you tomorrow," she said.

"Have a good root," I replied, raising a hand in the wave. She didn't have far to go, just the park a block over, where she'd sink her roots in and spend the day.

As for me, I wasn't quite done. I finished putting the receipts and cash into the safe, threw on my white lambs-wool jacket—Daddy's least favorite color—then locked up and began the walk home. Only a dozen or so blocks and, for a girl like me, not a problem.

Some days, I even welcomed the exercise.

The night seemed unusually still. The air hung, breathless and thick, not even a whisper of wind. Odd, considering the violent gusts from earlier. The usual sounds heard at a sleepy, almost four o'clock seemed muted. Not a car in sight, not a single howling dog, nor a hissing cat. It was kind of refreshing, actually.

Stuffing my hands in my pockets, I let my feet carry me home, the occasional thought of the dark-haired Auric keeping me company—and warm.

No matter how I tried, I just couldn't get him out of my mind. Talk about maddening.

A mess of emotions swirled within, the foremost being confusion and arousal. Despite his lack of interest, Auric had definitely lit a fire inside me, but he'd also made my warning bells ring. I needed to find out more about him. Why all his interest in the owner of Nexus? Something about him warranted further investigation. Just one problem. I had no idea who he was and where to look. He'd neglected to give me a last name, and according to him, he'd only come to the area recently. So where could I get the scoop on him and his friends?

Asking Daddy was an option. If Auric belonged to him, then he'd be able to give me the scoop; but asking for help, aside from all the deals that went with it, meant tipping my hand. I didn't want my dad to know I'd found someone who interested me. I wanted to form my own opinions on Auric as a man, without my father coloring my view of him or trying to tip the scales falsely in Auric's favor.

Thinking about Daddy, and his possible involvement, really made me wonder, for which team did Auric play? Contrary to popular belief, good and evil weren't the only states of being—the expression 'many shades of gray' totally applied here. While God and Satan happened to be the biggest known players—and brothers, to boot—other powerful entities also existed. Did Auric work for one of them? Could I be any more paranoid?

As I walked in this silent, dead night, I pondered so many things, my thoughts weaving and losing themselves among the pathways of my slightly twisted mind. Yet, even distracted, I heard the soft thud of something hitting the ground behind me and the acrid aroma of brimstone.

My hands went for my side, but I had no sword.

The human authorities didn't allow people to wear them in public. And my ankles and thighs were weapon free. In my rush to get to work, and my complacency in this world, I'd forgotten them.

Shit. *I hope this doesn't cost me.*

CHAPTER THREE

No need to panic. A lack of an edged weapon didn't mean I was defenseless. I still had my body.

And, no, I wasn't talking about offering it for sex.

I could fight. Turning, body braced and ready for some hand-to-hand combat, I almost laughed to see a hellhound instead of something actually dangerous. One of my dad's less-than-stellar—AKA dumb—creations, which had escaped from the pit.

The beast growled at me and wagged its stub of a tail. Did I forget to mention I'd grown up with the hellhounds? Up until the age of twelve, they'd been my full-time guardians. Approach me with any kind of ill intent and my canine friends didn't need dinner.

They might be dumb, but they were loyal to a

fault. I totally adored them. Of course, being fond didn't mean I could leave a killing machine from the pit roaming the human world. After all, we were talking hellhound here. The good news was, this one wore a collar inscribed with its name. That meant all it would take was a few words, a little oomph of power, and I could send it back to Hell—and then call the Hound Master and give him shit for not taking care of my puppies.

Before I could lean forward and read the tag for its name, strong hands gripped me and pulled me sideways into an alley.

I'll admit I let out a girl scream. "What the fuck?" Okay, so maybe not so girly. Then again, I was startled. Who was stupid enough to grab me, and how had I missed their approach?

"You can thank me later," said a familiar, gravelly voice.

"Thank you for what, dirtying my coat?" I stared at the smear of dirt across my sleeve, the fault of the dumpster I'd brushed against when he yanked me into the alley.

"Well, excuse me." Cue the superbly drawled sarcasm. "Next time, I'll let the hellhound tear you into bite-sized chunks."

"Oh, please. They wouldn't dare." Too late, I

realized how odd that sounded; and judging by the way his brows shot up, he caught my snafu.

Releasing my arms, he stepped back, a quizzical expression on his face.

I went on the attack to distract him from my words. "Why are you following me? What are you, some kind of freak stalker?"

"If by stalking you mean protecting. I saw a pretty girl walking by herself and decided to follow at a safe distance to make sure she got home all right. Good thing I did."

My heart fluttered. He'd called me pretty. He'd wanted to protect me. How cute—but so unnecessary. "I appreciate the thought behind it, but really, I can take care of myself."

"Even against hellhounds?" His brow arched with understandable skepticism.

"Piece of cake," I boasted. That wasn't, technically, giving anything away. Lots of special folk could take care of hellhounds. And dammit, even if I'd passed my airhead course, that didn't mean I felt comfortable practicing it.

Sometimes I hated having to hide who I was and what I could do. Did I really want Auric to think I was a useless twit in need of saving?

Why did I care what he thought was the better question?

"I don't think I've ever heard of anyone referring to hellhounds as a piece of cake. Just who and what are you?" His questions were getting repetitive.

I rolled my eyes. "I told you, my name is Muriel."

Auric crossed his arms over his chest—did I mention he had a really broad chest?—and gave me a stern look.

Oh, please, once Satan gave you 'the look,' all other looks paled in comparison. I just glared right back at him until he sighed with evident exasperation—another sound I was familiar with.

"I give up with you. If you think hellhounds are so easy, why don't you take care of it then?" He swept his hand to the alley entrance and smirked.

He smirked at me! I was torn between wiping it off his face and kissing it. What could I say? He really had my lusty side wrapped around his...*big finger*.

I chose to do nothing. Did I mention I didn't like choices? Without waiting to see if Auric followed, I spun on my heel—these ankle boots I'd found on a discount rack were divine—and stalked back to the puppy–er, beast.

Things had turned interesting during my verbal spat with Auric.

My sweet misunderstood puppy had put on a few pounds in my absence, a bulking mechanism they resorted to when they felt threatened. As to the threat, it would seem my earlier observations about Auric's companions were correct.

A golden panther hissed and swiped at the growling hound, using its body to keep the dog from reaching me. Even if I'd moved out, the hounds still seemed to retain a protective instinct where I was concerned. But my poor puppy wasn't just being taunted by a large cat. Mr. Smooth Talking Blue-eyes held a staff aloft and chanted.

I wanted to shake my head. Why did wizards always go for the long, drawn-out spells? Hadn't they learned yet that fancy spells meant a higher probability of death? Which, on second thought, was probably a good thing. A form of population control: survival of the fittest. But I was getting off track.

Thus far, Auric's two friends didn't look too banged up, and thankfully, they hadn't dented the hellhound either. My puppies from the pit were so misunderstood.

I'll save you, furbaby.

"Get out of the way," I demanded.

The bloody cat didn't move, and the wizard kept chanting.

Such a lack of respect on this plane. There were times I could understand why my daddy felt a need to lay a medieval smackdown. Times like these.

Ignore me and scare my poor snarling and rabid hellhound? Not on my watch. First problem, a certain feline. Easy enough. I yanked the kitty's tail and slapped it on the ass. "Shoo!" As it spun and yowled, I stepped around it, ignoring its indignant look.

"Next time move," I muttered as I knelt in front of the hound. I held out my hands. "Come here, baby."

"What is she doing?" the wizard asked, finally interrupting his boring chant.

Doing? I was showing them how a woman took care of a problem. And did it right.

My dog ignored me, choosing to instead snarl at the golden cat eyeing us from the side.

"I said come here." Fingers outstretched, I uttered the command "come" in ancient Aramaic. Only one of the many tongues I knew. Of course, the one I'd been dying to try was French, but that would have to wait for another day.

The hound, with its glowing red eyes, which

reminded me of home, slunk to me on its belly. Then rolled onto its back for a scratch. I couldn't resist the short, stubby fur and scrubbed a few times. Then scratched some more as I spotted the look on Auric's face.

"Are you seriously giving a hellhound a belly rub?"

"And kisses too," I said as I leaned over to snuggle its snout. "Maybe next time, before you attack, try a little love."

"It's a hellhound."

"Exactly. A hound. Someone's pet," I said, my admonishment clear. "Maybe it wandered away from its owner. That's not a reason to kill it." I ignored Auric in favor of the dog. "Off you go, and no more chasing plasma balls to the mortal side." Touching the tip of my fingers to the coal black nose of the dog, I said its name and the Aramaic word for home. With a wag of its tail, the beast faded, on its way back to the pit, and safety.

I stood amidst applause.

I bowed. It seemed only right.

"Bravo," said Auric, still clapping. "That was utterly fantastic."

"And much easier than your plan."

"Maybe."

"Maybe?" I couldn't help a quirk of my lips.

It was met by a smile and a kick to the stomach. Okay, not a real kick, more like an emotional one, but still. When Auric decided to put those lips to work, he packed quite the punch.

"How did you banish the beast with only two simple words?" asked Lothario, interrupting our staring match. "Are you a witch? Or a demon?" The staff he angled my way almost made me giggle.

"I'm neither. I'm just—um—special." That was only a tad of an understatement.

The seriously gorgeous blond panther became human again, and, shaking his hair out of his eyes, said, "That was cool." His deep voice still made me shiver, and I eyed his naked, well-muscled body with interest. Tall, lean, not an ounce of fat on him, but definitely some girth where it counted.

A view obstructed by a certain tall and grumpy fellow.

"Do you mind? I was enjoying the view." Actually, I was enjoying it more now that Auric showed signs of jealousy, or did he get that tic by his eye and the tight jaw every time his friend got naked? Maybe I had the jealousy wrong...

I was about to ask which team he played for when a certain boisterous yodel stopped me dead. "Yoo–hoo! Muriel. I was hoping I'd bump into you, and there you are."

Fuck.

CHAPTER FOUR

BRACE YOURSELF AND LOCK UP YOUR MEN. Seriously. Lock. Up. Your Guy. Girl. Or whatever it was that you banged because my half-sister Bambi, and, no, that wasn't just her stage name, was sashaying up the street.

In my case, I didn't have a hole big enough to drop in the three hunks I was playing with, which meant they were goners. No one could resist a succubus. And Bambi was one of the most powerful ones ever. One only had to look at her and...

Well, peek for yourself. Imagine voluptuous blonde, a little over five foot six, with ridiculous hourglass curves—which she assured me I could have, too, if I'd just wear one of the zillion damned corsets she'd gotten me. Um, no. I was fine with my normal set of curves and a waist that was bigger than a hand's span.

It wasn't just her shape that drew the eyes—and lust—of those around her. She knew how to frame it so it proved even more tempting. Her skirt dipped just low enough to cover her crotch, and every so often flashed the white cotton of her panties. Contrary to what some stories might want you to think, there was nothing more tempting to a man than simple, white, innocent cotton panties.

Seduction wasn't my goal, though, I wore them because they were comfortable, but I was straying from my point. We were talking about my sister's get-up. Red stilettos to extend the length of her legs, and a rhinestone halter-top that molded to her perky tits and showed off her hand-swallowing cleavage.

With that kind of outfit, was it any wonder she drew the male eye? So much for attracting Auric. With my blond succubus sister on the scene, I'd be lucky if I didn't get trampled when the guys tripped over themselves trying to meet her.

Or not.

I found myself surprised. Auric and his friends only spared a quick glance at my sister. The naked shapeshifter turned his back and busied himself with a pile of clothes. The wizard tapped his staff on the ground, an interesting trick that shrank it to pocket-sized.

Bambi laughed, a husky chuckle. "Well, that's a first. A man shrinking his wood and keeping it in his pocket."

A lame innuendo for my usually suave sister, but I didn't spare her a glance. How could I when Auric still had his eyes on me?

Me. Not my sister.

Ignoring Bambi earned him big brownie points because it wasn't easy finding a guy who managed to pass the sister test. See, it wasn't as if I hadn't been in lust or like before. It'd happened quite a few times, but before I made the ultimate decision to indulge in the horizontal tango, I set all of my previous boyfriends to one simple task. I introduced them to Bambi.

A few passed, only to fail later. How interesting that Auric and his friends ran the succubus gauntlet and had won, but honestly, the only one I really cared about was Auric. He was the one I was seriously in lust with.

This didn't mean I'd be jumping his bones—yet. I still didn't trust him, not to mention he still had some more tests to pass. But so far, I had to admit being impressed. After all, Bambi was hot, smokingly so, and he barely spared her a glance. Suspicious, I threw some lures at him. "That's my sister, Bambi, in case you're wondering."

"That's nice," he said, still watching me and taking a step closer. His body hovered close enough to mine that I could feel the heat radiating from him. Or was it me? Either way, it was getting hot out here.

"She's single," I said helpfully.

"Are you?" he retorted.

My breath started coming a little faster as he inched even closer to me and invaded my personal space, close enough I had to look up at him. "I'm single," I whispered, caught by his green eyes.

"So am I." He leaned down.

I closed my eyes and...suddenly found myself being yanked to the side.

"Come on, Muriel. We've got to be going. Say goodbye," said Bambi, in her smoky voice that would have made big bucks on a phone-sex line.

A really big part of me wanted to dig my heels in and protest. *He was going to kiss me. And she ruined it.* It made me so mad.

So...shit. The fact that I wanted it so badly made me do...nothing. I let my sister lead me away.

I barely knew the guy; why on earth would I let him kiss me? So he checked off a few boxes on my list for *the one*. Big deal. Still plenty more items for him to fail.

And the bigger question remained, just who and what was he? I still didn't quite buy his 'I was following you to protect you' crap. He'd pumped me too hard for info at the bar. He was after something, and I wasn't conceited enough to think it was just my sweet ass.

I wouldn't put it past him to have devised a new ploy to get information, like seduce the bartender so she'd spill her secrets. Well, he'd have to try a lot harder then. My hormones screamed, "Yay!" Apparently, they weren't averse to him trying to get me to melt again.

"I'll be seeing you again," he shouted.

Notice how he didn't ask, when he assumed it would happen. I couldn't help but add a little more wiggle to my step, a rapid step as my sister dragged me up the street. After a block, she finally slowed her pace and let go of her iron grip on my arm.

"Damn, that's some grip," I complained as I rubbed the sore spot.

"I've been working out a lot at the bordello getting ready for the annual Jerk Off."

And, yes, that was as perverted as it sounded. I'd never gone. Some things I really didn't need to see.

"What the hell was that pussyblock back there?"

"What makes you think I wasn't just looking out for my little sister?"

"Because if you thought I was gonna get laid, you would have ordered a pizza, sat down, and watched."

"Only to be sure you hadn't forgotten anything in Cherry Popping 101."

"How could I forget?" I'd tried. Nothing erased the videos. Oh damn, the videos... Sob.

"Did anything happen before I arrived?"

Somehow I didn't think she was talking about anything so benign as the dog. "A giant orgy. Me and all three guys in the alley."

Bambi laughed.

I frowned. "What's so freaking funny?"

"The thought of you in a ménage." She snickered. "Anyone who waits for true love isn't going to get into bed with a bunch of guys."

Funny how her words sounded so ominous to me.

"Fine. So I didn't get freaky with them. That doesn't explain you suddenly coming to the rescue."

"Dad."

Daddy dear. Of course. The meddling fool. "Why?"

She shrugged. "I'm not sure because he never

really did say. Although he was quite adamant. He didn't care that I was in the midst of giving a pair of twins a reverse lap dance, ready to suck some life force for dinner. Dad called and told me to get my ass over to your bar and walk you home."

"He didn't say why?" I'd have thought Dad would have been excited to see me finally showing an interest in someone. Apparently, there was something about Auric and his friends he didn't like. Being a proper rebellious daughter, that, of course, made them hotter.

"No, he didn't give a reason, and I didn't ask. Not all of us are brave enough to question when *he* gives orders," she replied dryly.

"Oh, please, Dad just talks tough; deep down inside, you know he loves us." Spoken with the utmost confidence.

Bambi started choking and coughing. I pounded her on the back.

"Oh, by the hag's hairy tit," Bambi wheezed. "You're special, Muriel."

"Thank you." I liked to think I was special, too.

We arrived at my apartment building, but Bambi stopped me before I went inside.

"One second before you go, lamb. I'm curious, about that guy you almost kissed. Do you like him?"

Question of the night. One I still didn't have an answer for. "I don't know. I just met him. He's hot, though." So hot he made me want to rip his clothes off, cover him in chocolate, and lick him all over. Distracted, I almost missed what Bambi said.

"Listen, for what it's worth, I super aimed my succubus power at him."

She tried to whammy him, and it had failed.

I didn't need the raise of her brows to grasp the significance. Auric hadn't just passed the test; he'd passed with better than flying colors. The realization stuck with me as she hugged me and then walked away, her voluptuous ass swinging.

The distraction her revelation provided helped me as I trudged up the stairs to my penthouse flat. Ha. Fourth floor walkup closet was more like it, but it was an excellent source of exercise, not to mention cheap on rent.

Who was Auric? Bambi had sicced all her powers on Auric, and he'd resisted her. He was something special.

Was he the one?

I might never know because chances were I'd never see him again; after all, this was the first time I'd ever seen him and his friends in my bar. Unless I was right about him being after something, in which case he'd probably return to pump me or the staff for more info.

Or he might come back just to see me. My hopeful inner voice needed a slap. Yet, the hope persisted. It clung to me, even as I undressed for bed and washed my face. I couldn't help but wonder if he'd come back again the next day and give me the kiss he'd almost planted on me earlier.

What would it have felt like? His lips caressing mine, his big hands pulling me close...

I shivered at the thought, a tremor that quickly turned into sensual longing. An arousal that had grabbed me in its clutches and refused to let go since I'd set eyes on him. Thankfully, I'd never claimed to be a good girl.

People might wonder—or outright ask, like my dad and sister—how I resisted sex. I made no bones about the fact that some guys just totally turned me on. I was human—maybe, or was that fractionally? I had needs. Some I could handle myself.

Now, some folks eschewed masturbation. Some blah blah blah about saving themselves for a lover. It was shameful. Dirty.

That reasoning only served to heighten my arousal and had me eagerly shedding my panties. They dropped into a white cotton puddle at my feet.

Naked, I flopped onto my mattress. The bounce never failed to make me giggle. As I nestled into my plush duvet, I pulled my knees toward my chest and spread them. Possibly not the sexiest look, but very accessible.

Licking a finger to moisten it, I touched myself. Down there. And it felt good.

The nub of my clitoris was so ready for a touch. One quick stroke, and I was squirming. How I loved the way it made my body feel.

My slick finger worked my clit back and forth. Oh yes. That felt good, so good. The only way I imagined it could get better was if someone else touched me.

Not just any someone.

Auric.

Thinking his name brought to mind his face. Such a sigh-worthy face. Those hard lips, that square jaw. What would that short stubble, which would appear by morning, feel like as it rubbed against my skin.

Friction. Mmm... How I wanted to feel it for real.

Just like I wanted to feel his lips, for real, not just in a kiss but the ultimate pleasure. Imagine Auric going on a sensory trip using only his lips on my body.

Oh.

As my nipples puckered in delight and my body undulated on the bed, I wondered at the moist heat of his mouth if it latched on. As he sucked, would he watch me with those wicked green eyes? Would he bite my pointed buds? Shudder. Honey moistened my nether lips, giving me all the natural honey I needed to keep playing.

Tonight I was feeling dirty though. It wasn't enough to just touch myself. To rub my slick clit. I needed something a little more. My vibrator wasn't long, but it was thick. It was a dangerous toy because the trick was to keep it outside of me.

The length of it vibrated, a soft quiver that made me hiss in pleasure as I ran it over my clitoris and then on to my sex.

That was nice, but even nicer if I seesawed it back and forth, letting it thrum against my swollen bud then against my pussy, which ached.

How I ached. Ached to fill that void within me. Could Auric be the man?

It didn't take much imagination to place Auric above me, Auric with his hard cock, rubbing against me. Teasing me. Was he a teasing lover?

Would he prove rough or gentle? *Both please.*

Would he take charge and tell me what to do to please him, or would his focus be on me and bringing me pleasure? *Both again!*

Would he lick my sweet nectar, his face buried between my thighs?

A shudder went through me, and I felt the tension coiling within me. My breathing became fast and panting.

I pushed the plastic aid hard against me, not inside, never inside. Even flushed with passion, I was careful. The forbidden helped the tease.

Gyrating my hips, I bit my lip as I imagined Auric over me, covering me with his big body, making me vulnerable to him. The head of him would push at my sex, looking to penetrate. Fill me. Claim me...

With a gasp, I came, ripples of pleasure going through me, rocking and rolling me, a bliss more intense than usual.

My body practically glowed with power. Something about sex really seemed to excite the esoteric part of me.

It was short-lived though, as was my pleasure. For the first time, it wasn't enough.

My arousal returned as the phantom image of Auric still beckoned me. My body, make that my whole being, was hungry for something other than the little titillation I could give it.

I wanted to fuck.

Correction. I wanted to fuck Auric.

I needed to.

What did that mean? Was I finally ready to forgo my vow of 'no sex until I found love'? Had my body finally had enough?

Mutiny in my pussy.

Not happening, dammit. I refused to let my hormones win. My horniness had nothing to do with needing Auric or any other guy giving me cock. I didn't need cock. I had nimble fingers.

I was obviously just a little more aroused than usual. No problem. I'd just masturbate again.

The second time round, I was out to prove a point. I played rougher with my body, but I liked it. Liked it too much as I imagined Auric roughly taking me and... Oh. That orgasm arrived quicker than expected.

Maybe its quickness was why I still felt a quiver in my slick sex. I caressed myself again and, with my eyes shut, fantasized about Auric kissing me. Auric fucking me. Auric loving me...

Yes! Yes! Yes! Another O, and still I felt dissatisfied.

Fuck. And my pussy was too sore for another encore. The cold pack on my crotch, though, at least had the effect of chilling my libido.

But it did nothing to help my mind. As I drifted into a tired slumber, I still hadn't decided what to do about Auric and the effect he had on my body.

I did, however, make one decision. I'd definitely have to see him again. Maybe if I spent some time with him, I'd realize he was just a man—a flawed mortal creature—and my body would lose this obsessive desire to be claimed by him.

You'll never lose this feeling because he is the one.

Who'd said that?

CHAPTER FIVE

THE NEXT DAY DAWNED ALL TOO EARLY.
Seriously, could someone get the sun to get up at like
say ten, maybe eleven?

But unfortunately Ra, the bloody sun god, was
some kind of early-waking freak. The type that
jumped out of bed and went jogging. Much like the
snooze button, you had an urge to kill the bastard so
you could get ten more minutes of sleep.

I was trying to cut down on my killing, though.
So the sun rose and dragged me with it.

Brilliant yellow sunshine flooded my room, and I
couldn't help but blink and peer out of squinty eyes.
The smart thing would have been to install some
heavy-duty blinds, but that involved me, a drill, and
measuring.

I had my strengths. Hanging stuff wasn't one of them.

A jaw-cracking yawn and a stretch didn't clear the fuzzies in my mind. Yet, despite my cloudy head, my body thrummed with energy. Odd.

My sleep was spent in vivid dreamscape, but I wasn't alone. Guess who was there with me.

In my dream, Auric and I were both normal human beings. Key word, normal. Nothing supernatural or special about us. We went on dates. We talked. We made love in bed, in the park, on the washing machine... The perfect life. The perfect fantasy that, when recalled in the light of day, seemed so impossibly unreal.

Aspiring to a normal life was for someone in deep denial. I was Lucifer's daughter. I would never, ever live a mundane existence.

Fist pump.

I'd hate to wither away from boredom.

A little spice in one's life kept things interesting. While a certain masculine enigma kept things horny. Damn but I had it bad for Auric. Perhaps I should think about having myself checked for spells. Just because I repelled most created magic didn't mean I was entirely immune. Magic came in many flavors. I repelled only a certain shade of it.

Had he cast a lust spell on me?

It would explain why I still felt so damned horny. My poor pussy chafed from the number of times I'd rubbed it last night, trying to erase this attraction I couldn't shake. Utterly out of control, a totally new feeling for me. It both excited and scared me. Could I be falling in love? Did I even believe in love at first sight?

I'd never felt so confused—and aroused—in my life. And I didn't like it one bit.

Deciding exercise might succeed where masturbation hadn't, I dressed in a pink track suit with a black stripe, grabbed my iPod, and headed out for a jog.

As my feet pounded the pavement in a rhythmic cadence, I let myself fall into the trance that exercising always brought. I'd discovered this soothing mind trick years ago when I'd first started jogging as a way to keep in shape. As Satan's daughter, I never dared show weakness; and the ability to outrun situations had, on more than one occasion, served me well.

Eyes unseeing, I ran the trail in the park, the songs of the eighties that I loved so much blasting in my ears. Out of the corner of my eye, I caught a flicker of motion, another jogger moving faster about to pass me. I moved over to the edge of the lane, which is the only reason why the blade aimed at me missed, but I heard the almost silent whistle of it.

In less than a heartbeat, I'd pivoted to the side and confronted a stranger with glowing eyes. Yellow eyes, which probably indicated some kind of shifter. Demons tended toward the red.

My assailant twirled his blade, dodging in for another strike. He should have run.

With a grace I'd learned in ballet and tae kwon do, my foot arced up, tilted, and kicked the hand holding the knife. My attacker hissed in pain and dropped into a half-crouch, fists flying. I ducked and dodged with ease then jabbed back with a hard smack to the bridge of his nose. He reeled back in pain, blood spurting, and at this point a smart mugger would have moved on and looked for easier prey. But there was a reason this idiot had turned to a life of crime.

Instead of hotfooting it, his form rippled as he shifted into something that seemed to have a lot of teeth. Something I learned at a young age—things with lots of teeth bite.

Since the whole trying-to-chew-your-arm-off thing tended to hurt, I took off sprinting. Getting into a fight, even if I had a pair of blades strapped to my thighs, was never the right recourse when in public. Too many people ready to shoot a video and post it on the Net.

My plan: make it to a populated location and lose him. Anyone that wouldn't pass the humanity test took care not to be noticed, lest the government start hunting us. Or, even worse, according to the movies, dissect us.

The only problem with my plan? I'd reached the location in the trail that loomed the farthest from civilization. Should I stand and fight?

How about cursing myself for being an idiot? I'd gotten so complacent in my new normal life that I'd forgotten about the people hunting me. I tried to pretend I belonged here and fit in. I did the things everyday mortals did, like going to work and jogging on the trails. All that could end in an instant if someone happened to videotape me skinning the cat.

If I were in Hell, I wouldn't have hesitated. I loved fur, especially on my naked body.

But this world frowned on natural clothing, preferring machine-made, sweat-shop fabrics. My father loved the irony. *"They'll march and scream about the rights of animals, and yet they'll consume the products made by children in appalling situations."*

However, who cared about the fate of the mortal plane's textile industry? If I didn't move my fat ass— no amount of squats was taking away that little jiggle —then my days in this world could end up numbered.

And I'd have to move back home and listen to my daddy's "Told you so."

Legs pumping to the tune 'She's a Maniac,' I tore through the woods, my running speed faster than a regular human's, but not fast enough to outrun a shifter. While I didn't feel its animal breath on my neck, I could sense the energy of the beast as it gained on me, a hungry force on the case, getting closer and closer.

Fuck it. I wouldn't outrun it, and it wouldn't give up.

I stopped and turned to face the creature that hunted me, fingers crossed no one was watching. But just in case, I didn't draw my knives yet.

A large mountain cat bounded down the forested trail, cougar I'd wager, and not the divorcee kind with a bit of money and a huge sexual appetite.

Long canines peeked from its muzzle whilst its eyes glowed with menace.

Bring it.

I'd never wrestled weaponless with a beast before, so I quickly came up with a plan of attack. One, don't let it eat me. I heard being digested sucked, or so the damned who'd survived it claimed. Step two in my plan, keep the claws away from the face. Vanity all the way. In case someone took pictures, I wanted to look my best.

Part three of my plan, the best part, kick some ass! Or was that tail? Whatever. Emerge triumphant and not ruin my most recent manicure.

Legs slightly apart, knees bent, I braced myself for some hand-to-claw combat with an oversized cat.

The tawny beast slowed its approach, crouching down low, his belly almost to the ground in a slow slink.

I yawned. "Would you hurry it up? I'm due for my late morning latte."

It snarled.

Amateur.

I snarled back.

That had him recoiling, but only for an instant. The cougar coiled his haunches, ready to pounce on me. It drew its muzzle back in an impressive show of teeth and— Got slammed to the side as a large, golden body shot out of the woods. With a screech of rage, the two large beasts, locked in a fur-and-fang battle, went rolling off into the woods.

"Well, that was unexpected," I muttered.

"Is it me, or does trouble seem to follow you?" said a gravelly voice.

CHAPTER SIX

NO WAY. IT COULDN'T BE HIM.

Not believing my luck, I turned around, only to confront the man of my dreams—and masturbation fantasy.

He looked just as delicious dressed in jogging pants and a T-shirt that bulged over well-defined biceps. Bearing a slight sweat and his face annoyingly arrogant, I still found him breathtakingly gorgeous. I didn't know if I should prepare to fight him or throw him to the ground and maul him. Maybe I'd gotten lucky and he'd come to maul me.

"Stalking me again?" I asked, instead of obeying my body's instincts.

"Nope, pure luck or mischance, depending on how you look at it."

I doubted Uncle Lucky had a hand in this. Something about it smelled much too contrived.

"I am going to assume that the other furry fellow was your friend from yesterday?" I said, gesturing to the woods, which had gone quiet.

"Yup."

"You're not worried about him getting caught on camera?"

"Nope. Chris has a spell fucking with electronics in these woods. It should hold long enough for this to get resolved."

"Resolved as in..."

"The less you know, the better."

Seriously? Was that all he was going to say? I crossed my arms, arched my brow, and waited for him to elaborate.

It usually worked on the minions in Hell.

Not him. He waited right back.

The snarls in the forest died off. Silence reigned, and it drove me batty. "Aren't you going to see if he's all right?" I finally exclaimed.

"Nope."

Auric really took the strong, silent type a bit too far. "Since you're not worried, I'll just be off then. Bye." I turned away from him and started walking away.

Auric wouldn't be shaken that quickly, though, and caught up to me. "Why was that shifter attacking you?"

"Maybe I smelled good," I said. Actually, I had no idea why it had chosen to come after me. Random act of violence was my assumption. Women got attacked every day. Perhaps I happened to be in the wrong place at the wrong time.

Although, given my attacker's special abilities, it wasn't much of a stretch to wonder if the encounter was intentional. And not unheard of. Just another of many attempts to kill Lucifer's daughter.

With the danger passed, I felt a little gypped. Since we never got to fight, I had to wonder who would have won the battle—the cat-man or me?

Duh. Me.

"You think it liked your smell?"

"Or my ass." I peeked over my shoulder. "What do you think?"

"I think you enjoy changing the subject."

"And you ask a lot of questions," I retorted. A little annoyed that he didn't check out my awesome glutes or compliment them, I fired back. "How do you expect me to know what the shifter wanted? It's not like we stopped to have a conversation. I was a tad too busy, fighting for my life."

"Fighting for your life?" Auric chuckled. "Exaggerate much?"

"What are you implying?"

"Not implying, but stating, that even if we hadn't come along, you'd have come out just fine, but I wouldn't say the same for that feline."

He thought I had skills. Now, that made me feel good, which, in turn, made me suspicious. A compliment about my ability to take care of myself from the same man who'd claimed I needed protection last night. Why the sudden about-face?

"Just what is your game?" I asked. "You came into the bar last night asking me all kinds of questions about the bar and its owner. You followed me home, and then in the mother of all coincidences, you happen to be on-hand when some freak shifter I've never seen before attacks me out of the blue. If you ask me, that's an awful lot of weird coincidences, and I'm starting to wonder if perhaps you're up to something." Nefarious. And naked.

If you asked me, the bad boys of the world needed to get a little looser with their clothes when committing vile acts.

"No game, no ulterior motive." Lie. I could spot those a mile away. "I went to your bar because of a recommendation." True, but hiding something.

"Sorry if my questions made you uncomfortable." No, he wasn't. "I was curious and simply making conversation." Instead of trying to get me into bed. "As for last night, yes, I intentionally followed you to protect you. It's just who I am."

Who he was? Ha. Half of what he told me was a lie baked in partial truths. The mystery around him deepened. "Whatever," was my brilliant riposte.

His head turned a moment before I heard it. The faint sound of someone coming up the trail on two feet.

Was it his naked friend? Ooh. I craned for a peek around him. But he wasn't very obliging, and he blocked my view.

"Listen, Muriel, I want to clear up this misconception you have about me. Why don't you have dinner with me?"

Dinner? Or a chance to work me over one-on-one? He could torture me all he wanted. And I wanted. I wouldn't give in—but I'd enjoy.

Alas...his invitation had only one answer. "I have to work." Such a responsible business owner. My dad hated it.

"What about a coffee before work? Say in one hour?"

A negative shake of my head. I didn't have

enough time, not if I was going to do a supplies run for the bar first. But my body wouldn't let him go that easily, and it took over my mouth. Mutiny! "Why don't you come to the bar tonight? You can walk me home, intentionally this time, and protect me from the bogeyman."

As soon as I was done making the invitation, I almost bit my tongue. Treacherous, horny body. But I couldn't take it back now. I'd look weak.

Besides, apparently Auric liked my solution because another of his rare smiles graced his face, a big one. The effect it had on my equilibrium shocked me. I sucked in a breath. A tingling warmth spread from my head to my toes, and I became especially tingly in between.

"Sounds good. I'll see you tonight, then."

Ominous and yet exciting.

While we'd been talking, we'd reached the edge of the woods. In the distance, I could see people and vendors—in other words, safety. I turned to say goodbye, but Auric had already left, jogging back down the trail, more than likely to meet up with his friend. A friend who had gone furry in public to save me. If I didn't already have the hots for Auric, I might have been tempted to get to know his friend better.

But who needed a shy blond when I had a chance with Mr. Arrogance himself?

We had a date of sorts tonight. A date that might involve petting. Touching. I had to look my best. Provide some access for groping without being too easy to remove.

Oh the dilemma. What would I wear?

CHAPTER SEVEN

Normally, I had no problem choosing an outfit for work, and normally, I wasn't a ball of nerves because I wanted to impress a guy without looking as if I was trying to impress him.

I had a clothing tantrum like I'd not had since my high school years when I went through that phase where I insisted on wearing jeans and sweat shirts instead of short plaid skirts, knee-high, socks, and a tied-off white blouse. My sister Bambi was so put out that I wouldn't wear what she got me. Thankfully, by the time grade twelve came around, along with my breasts, I'd come out of my don't-give-a-shit casual phase into my look-at-me one.

For a moment, I considered calling my sister for help, but I could just imagine her recommendation. Shortest skirt and sheerest blouse.

But I didn't want to go for the provocative, take-me-now look. Yet, I did want to look sexy. Just not too sexy or he'd think I liked him. Which I did, but I didn't want to come across as too slutty or desperate.

Frustrated with my emotional seesawing, I finally settled on black slacks that belled at the cuffs, paired with a gold lamé blouse that shimmered and, when left unbuttoned partway, gave just the right hint of cleavage. Elegantly attractive—with a really good bra.

Since I didn't want to have any wind/hair incidents today, I pulled my long hair up on the sides and clipped it in place with an oversized barrette. It had the advantage of keeping my long locks out of my face yet leaving it loose and flowing down my back.

A coating of glam makeup, a daub of perfume on my wrists and behind my ears, and *voila*, I was ready for my work/date.

I made it to the bar on time without running into any hot men. Yeah, I was disappointed.

If my staff noticed me watching the door that night like a hawk, they wisely gave no sign of it. It was like being a teenager again—breathlessly waiting with my hands clammy and my tummy a swirl of butterflies.

Time passed, and I waited. And waited some more. And...

That panty-teasing bastard never showed up. I called myself all kinds of stupid as I emptied the registers, stowed the receipts, and wiped down the counter. Apparently, I'd put more stock and importance on this date than he had.

What a pathetic idiot. As I turned the key in the lock, shutting the bar for the night, I saw a shadow detach itself from the building, and my heart foolishly sped up, even as my hand itched to grab a knife and throw it.

Auric had come after all, and mixed with my elation, was an urge to kill him. He'd made me feel. Made me want. He made me wait. Um, hello, this princess of Hell waited for no one.

Especially not a man.

I turned my back on him.

Petty, which was probably why he laughed, a low chuckle that stroked parts of me that I didn't know could shiver.

"Now, baby, don't tell me you're going to be pissy 'cause I'm late. I got hung up or I'd have been here earlier."

"Me being pissy would imply I gave a damn whether you showed or not." I graced him with a cool smile that was at complete odds with my sizzling senses. "In case you weren't sure, I'm leaning toward the not."

His teeth flashed, brilliant white in the shadows. "Would it help if I said I made sure I'd arrive at closing time?" I would have forgiven him except he added, "I didn't want the streets to suffer if you walked alone."

Did he just imply I was dangerous?

A glance at him showed his lips twitching. Humor, a new facet to my knight in leather armor. I could live with a bit of humor in my life, especially given my oftentimes sarcastic attitude.

Deciding to accept his apology for the moment, I paid attention to other things such as the fact that he wore the same leather duster of the previous evening. Once again, I admired it—envy was a sin I did well.

Unable to resist, I reached out a hand and stroked the supple surface of his coat, feeling a thrill that my hand strayed so close to his actual body. "It's so soft," I murmured.

"Not for long, if you keep stroking it," he drawled.

It took me a second, but when I caught his unexpected sexual innuendo, I giggled. "That was so bad."

"Only if you're thinking dirty to start with." Uttered with a straight face. For a second I wondered if my insane desire for him had imbued sexual meaning into innocent words, but the twinkle in his eyes betrayed him, and I punched his arm.

"You jerk."

"Ow," he yelped.

"Serves you right for teasing me."

"You made it too easy."

Easy, too, was how quickly I forgave him. "I thought you'd forgotten about me." As soon as the words left my mouth, I wanted to kick myself for sounding so damn vulnerable. And pathetic.

Shoot me now.

"You're pretty hard to forget," he said with a smile. "Shall we? The night awaits." He swept me a courtly bow, marred only by the somewhat wicked smile creasing his lips, a naughty grin that shot a bolt of lust straight through me.

I am ready. For what I couldn't have exactly said, but it definitely included spending more time with Auric.

We began walking, and to my inner surprise and pleasure, he grabbed my swinging hand and held it. I looked at his strong hand holding my smaller one. His tanned skin contrasted nicely against mine, and his strength was evident in his grip. Strange, how such a simple touch could make me feel. For one, I felt delicate, not something I got to enjoy often. What about protected? Because I had no doubt he'd spring into action if someone threatened me. And my blood ran hot, feverish hot, especially between my legs.

"I should probably give you my address."

"Sixty-six Devil's Lane, apartment six."

"How did you know that?" I asked, a little surprised. I'd made sure I was unlisted so as to maintain my privacy.

"I followed you and your sister home last night to make sure you got there safe. But really, Muriel, apartment six, sixty-six Devil's Lane?" His eyes glinted with amusement as he looked down at me.

I had the grace to blush. "I know it sounds clichéd, but would you believe I got it at a discount because people kept claiming the address was unlucky?"

"Oh, I believe it. But what about you? Weren't you worried it would draw attention from unsavory sorts?"

"What do you mean by unsavory? If you mean I get more than my fair share of Jehovahs at the door, then yes." But it should be noted they stepped up their visits after the time I ran to answer in a towel then somehow managed to drop it as I was explaining I believed in all kinds of gods but wasn't about to worship just one unless they made an honest woman of me.

"I take it you had an uneventful night at work?"

"Well, we did have a coven of drunken witches singing 'I Will Survive', but that was painful for everyone, not just me."

Auric chuckled. "So, Muriel the bartender, do you still think I'm stalking you?"

"I certainly hope so," I said. At his startled look, I chuckled. "Doesn't every girl want a man to be obsessed with her? To follow her every move and shower her with attention?"

"Funny, I would have taken you for the type that went after what she wanted."

"You don't know me well enough to say that."

"Not yet, but I'd like to," he said softly. His thumb stroked the back of my hand, sending little electrical shocks of awareness through me.

My heart fluttered at his words, and like a princess in a fairytale, I could feel myself falling under his spell. I had to remind myself I was a princess of Hell and fuzzy, happy endings were for books, not girls like me.

Stay alert. Something still seemed off. This charming, smooth-talker did not resemble the rough-and-rude guy I'd taken him for when we initially met.

"How come the first night in the bar and in the park you seemed a lot more uncouth? Yet tonight, you're more..." I paused, looking for the right word. "Gentlemanly. Do you have a split personality or something?" I wouldn't judge if that were the case. Some of my best friends were psychos.

"I'm not taking medication or seeing a professional for my mental health. But I can see why you might be confused. The night I went to your bar, I'd gotten some not-so-pleasant news. The guys thought a drink would calm me down. I apologize if I seemed abrupt. I have a hard time sometimes connecting with people I don't know. Actually, my friends were quite surprised by how quickly I warmed up to you. It usually takes me a lot longer."

I didn't know what to say at this backward compliment. Nor did I know if I should trust it. Words were easily spoken—and broken.

When we arrived at my building, I found myself reluctant to see him go. I knew inviting him up would be irresponsible, but... Peering at him, I found myself tempted. As for him, he said nothing, just stared at me with his bright green eyes, his expression mysterious, as it was partially hidden in shadows.

What was it about this dark, mysterious man that drew me like an ice cream truck on a hot summer day? I had no excuses this time. It wasn't danger bringing us together. It wasn't a need to impress his friends. In the short time since we'd met, I'd already lost most of my earlier uneasiness. It helped he'd not asked me any further about who owned the bar. Perhaps it simply was small talk the first time we met.

This was now our what, third meeting, fourth if you counted the bump encounter, and I had to admit I enjoyed his company. My attraction to him was undeniable, and yet his very appeal frightened me —excited me.

Torn, I hesitated outside my door, knowing he should go, but wanting him to stay.

The silence between us stretched as we gazed upon each other. But did we really need words?

Apparently he came to the same conclusion because Auric let go of my hand to place both of his on my waist, pulling me toward him. As my heart thumped madly, I peered into his face, and I saw the flash of his eyes as his visage drew closer to mine. My eyes fluttered shut, and I tilted my face, offering my mouth.

Would he kiss me?

He has to.

I might possibly kill him if he didn't.

The warmth of his breath tickled me. His lips hovered so tantalizingly close. Then a whisper of a caress. Such a soft touch, yet it packed a mighty punch to my libido, making me gasp. His lips brushed across mine again, and he pulled me closer to his body, branding me with his heat. My arms slipped around his waist, and I shuddered at the feel of his hard body. His lips pressed harder against mine, the wet edge of his tongue teasing me. I parted my lips slightly...

"Auric!"

Someone shouted his name, and I wanted to scream at them to go away.

You are interrupting a kiss here!

Would growling and stamping my feet help the situation? Probably not. But I sure felt like expressing my displeasure.

I think Auric might have felt the same way because I heard him sigh. "Fuck."

I opened my eyes and saw him looking down at me ruefully.

"Tell your friend to go away," I whispered.

"He wouldn't have come to find me unless it was important."

Was he seriously choosing his bud over kissing me?

"Fine then," I said, not even trying to hide my miffed tone or body language. I also didn't bother with a goodbye; I just left, an exit marred when I fumbled my key in the lock.

Auric's strong hand folded around mine, steadying it. I opened the door, still refusing to look at him, but he put his arm across the doorway and blocked me from entering.

"I'll see you tomorrow," he promised before giving me a hard kiss on the lips.

I wanted to say "No, you won't," but he strutted off too quickly for my addled wits to retort.

Jerk. I rubbed my tingling lips. Good kisser. But still a jerk. I still couldn't believe he'd ditched me for his buddy. Talk about a low blow to my feminine ego. However, on the upside, he'd kissed me!

He likes me.

The knowledge helped a little, even as it confused me even more.

Tonight, unlike our other meetings, had been nice. No uncomfortable questions, no violence. Just more confusion on just what my feelings were for him. Like, dislike, lust... Lots of lust.

The skin on my hand still tingled from him holding it, an old-fashioned, courtly gesture that still surprised me. He didn't seem like a man who held hands. Or a man who'd joke. And I'd been wrong about his kisses, too. They didn't just feel good; they felt great. If I'd thought I was aroused the night before, tonight my body burned with it.

I locked the door to my apartment and stripped, to lie naked on my sheets. The friction of the material on my sensitive skin made me writhe. In a sense, it had probably been a good thing I hadn't invited him up. My hormones were completely out of control around him. I might have done something foolish—and pleasurable—I thought, as I twisted one of my nipples hard while my other hand slid down over my belly to delve between my thighs.

Would he think of me when he went home? Would his hand slide down his own body, to grip a rock-hard cock and stroke it?

My breath came faster, and my finger moved quickly. Would his balls grow tight as he rubbed his shaft? I moaned, a stab of desire making me slick. I fantasized some more, wondering if, as Auric masturbated, he would be thinking of me riding him, my breasts jigging over his face. Licking him, my tongue laving its way down his chest. Sucking him, his cock filling my mouth.

With a scream, I came, my juices wetting the sheet beneath me, the intensity of my orgasm surprising me.

I didn't like this power Auric had over my body, but I seemed helpless to stop it. Even as I thought his name, I felt the pleasure coiling again. Rub as I may, though, I couldn't seem to make it go away. I wanted to cry with frustration.

I feared there would be only one solution to my sexual dilemma. But, dammit, I'd put up a fight before I compromised the vow I'd made to myself.

Who was I kidding? Unless I invested in a really sturdy chastity belt and lost the key, I was afraid my virgin days were numbered.

I just hoped my dad didn't set off the fireworks again like he did when I got my first period.

CHAPTER EIGHT

"I FORBID YOU TO SEE HIM," MY FATHER commanded in a booming voice.

I stuck my head out of the bathroom where I was brushing my teeth. "See who?" I mumbled through a mouthful of foam.

"You know who I'm talking about. The man you were with last night. You are to stay away from him."

"Are you talking about Auric?" My father growled at the name. How fascinating. "Since when do you care who I see? And besides, wasn't it you, just the other day, who was bugging me to get laid?"

"I still wish you to defile yourself, but you will do so with anyone but him or his companions."

Why did my father want me to avoid Auric and his crew?

The light bulb in my mind shone bright with

understanding, and I laughed. "Wait, I get it. This is your version of reverse psychology. Tell me not to jump his bones, and being a properly defiant daughter, I will immediately."

"Are you accusing me of subterfuge to get my way?"

"Not accusing, stating."

"Don't get lippy with me. This is no joking matter. You will stay away from that male, or else." Dad punctuated his threat with a little hellfire in his eyes, a move that spooked most mortals, but hey, I wasn't your everyday mortal.

"Or else what?" A sassy reply, but only because I really had a problem with people telling me what I could do.

"Or I will take you back to Hell with me and ground you until you're one hundred."

"I'd like to see you try."

Dad flexed his fingers, and his eyes narrowed. "Don't tempt me. My legion is bored and would be delighted to provide guard detail for a bratty princess."

My mouth dropped open. "You wouldn't dare!"

"I would. And that's final."

I'd never seen my dad so adamant about something. Sure, he gave me rules and expected me to break them, but he'd never threatened to ground me before for defying him. Usually, he applauded my outright defiance.

Even if he did get really mad—like the time I posted on Hellbook that he wore a onesie, with feet and a forked devil tail—he never did truly punish me. Not because he didn't want to, but because he couldn't.

Sucker!

I might not know who my mother was—and attempting to think made my head hurt—but she'd left one whopping geas—also known as a spell or a curse. I thought it was marvelous that it prevented Dad from using a disciplinary hand on my bottom. Then again, a little pain was fleeting, but the methods my father had to use to punish me in its stead...some humiliations lasted a lifetime.

Some were pretty benign and even funny, like hiding my books when I'd get to the good part. Not so funny was ensuring my period started when I was wearing white slacks to school. I never said thank you to him again.

In the end, none of those physically harmed me. We wouldn't discuss the mental damage though. I liked to think of it as character building.

All bark, no true bite. That was my dad. Until now.

Something about Auric had his horns in a knot, and I had to say, I found myself intrigued. So of course I lied—which would have made Dad happy had he known—and told him what he wanted to hear while secretly plotting to find out more about Auric and, of course, meet with him again.

"Fine, I'll stay away. But in Auric's and his friends' defense, they were only trying to help me from the hellhound that came to visit me, and the shifter that attacked me in the park."

"My hounds would never hurt one of my own." He couldn't hide the affront in his expression.

"I know that and you know that, but they didn't. They thought they were being heroes." Kind of cute, when you thought of it. Mortals trying to save Lucifer's daughter.

"And what's this about a shifter? No one told me about a shifter attacking you."

"Guess your spies are getting lazy. It happened during a jog in the park. Don't worry. I had it mostly under control."

"You killed it?"

"Nah. Auric's buddy did while Auric asked me out."

My father growled, the steam that curled from his ears betraying his ire. "How did I not know about any of this?"

Ooh, he really sounded pissed. I didn't need to be a psychic to guess that some underlings would scream before the day was through for slacking off. Apparently, I wasn't the only one who'd gotten complacent on the mortal plane.

"I need to go," said my father abruptly. "I meant what I said, Muriel. Stay away from those men, *him* especially." With that last warning, my satanic father, with a wag of his finger, sliced open a portal to Hell. Before stepping through, he turned his head, a full one hundred and eighty degrees, to add, "Go forth and do wicked things in my name." With an evil laugh, that many tried to imitate, he returned to Hades, where heads would probably roll.

I flopped onto my couch and sighed. Now Dad had done it. Auric, already sexy and dangerous, had just become even hotter because my dad hated him. More than hated; he'd forbidden me.

Oh my, Auric certainly had my interest now. And I didn't care if I was succumbing to that dreaded reverse psychology. Temptation was the ultimate sin.

Only one problem with disobeying my dad—and

pleasing myself. I had no idea if I'd ever see Auric again. It was not as if we'd exchanged phone numbers the night before. However, he had said he'd see me today. But I had to wonder if he meant it. Did he even feel anything for me? Doubt wanted to dig its claws and chose to remind me of the fact he'd had such an easy time leaving me mid-kiss. How utterly ego-crushing.

A girl could only hope—ugh, instead of fixing the odds in my favor—that he'd show up again, which gave me problem number two. As soon as Auric appeared on the scene, Daddy's spies would run right back to the pit and tell him.

Damn. I'd be flaunting my disobedience if I flirted openly, which usually meant a pat on the back; but his threat of grounding me in Hell gave me pause.

How to work around this dilemma? Perhaps I could give Auric the cold shoulder. Play hard to get. Make Auric think I was still pissed about last night—which I was. Then my dad's spies could report my obedient behavior, and I'd force Auric to do something drastic. Something romantic, or maybe even chivalrous.

Is he the type to kidnap a reluctant damsel and seduce her into compliance?

I shivered deliciously. Oh, to feel his big hands on my body again. This time, with uninterrupted sexual intent. I wouldn't mind getting the full version of the kiss, too, which had been so rudely cut short. I had a feeling the chemistry between us would prove explosive.

With those thoughts in mind, I dressed for the night's work. Cropped midriff top in crimson, black yoga pants that hung low on my hips, not to mention molded my ass and thighs obscenely. To top it off, calf-high black suede boots with fringe on the back. Looking in the mirror, I decided against the bra and shrugged it off. I looked approvingly in the mirror as the nubs of my nipples hardened against the fabric and protruded enticingly.

Being a virgin didn't mean I didn't know how to dress like a tart; after all, when the most renowned succubus in the world was related to me, I tended to learn a thing or two about fashion. I also intended to make sure I had Auric's undivided attention tonight. No more ditching me for his bros. I freely admitted to being selfish. I wanted it to be all about me.

I brushed my long chestnut hair until it crackled and floated about me—I'd been blessed with a great head of hair and more than one guy had said they'd like to yank it. A light coat of makeup, a touch of eyeliner, a stroke of mascara, and a wet-looking lip gloss completed the look.

Grabbing my leather jacket and purse, I locked my door before I headed for work, and hopefully an encounter with my new wet fantasy.

Instead, I encountered a tentacle reaching for my ankle from the sewer. Stiletto-heeled boots didn't just look good. They stabbed escaped Styx monsters from Hell, too.

CHAPTER NINE

THIS NIGHT WAS A REPEAT OF THE PREVIOUS. ME constantly watching the stupid door into the bar.

Rowdy coven of witches. No tall, dark, and yummy.

A hooded vampire, his ghastly white skin peeking. Not my leather-clad hunk.

A trio of elves complaining that it reeked of brimstone in my place. I personally tossed them out and, under that guise, peeked up and down the street. My pathetic need to see him made me want to jab a cocktail umbrella in my eye.

I stabbed a cherry with it instead and tried to curb my disappointment. It was only, after all, eight o'clock. The night had barely begun.

Do your job. It was all I could really do, and it kept my mind from straying—too often.

I couldn't have timed it better if I'd planned to. I'd just bent over to pick up a napkin that had fluttered to the floor when he walked in.

How did I know? Call it instinct—call it hormones. I didn't care; all I knew was my ass, which had been described as perfectly heart-shaped by more than one drunken supernatural, was sticking up in the air when he arrived.

Did I straighten right away? And fail at Wily Seduction 104, taught by my very own sister?

Nope, I stayed bent over and wiggled a little as I wiped at an imaginary spot. Between my legs, I could see the approach of his black motorcycle boots. He stopped less than two feet behind me. Not one to waste an advantage, I gave my butt a little shake before I straightened up, my hair swinging in an arc to settle in organized disarray, not an easy look to achieve.

"Hey, baby."

Shiver.

Must. Fight. Urge. To. Melt.

Not easy when he used that tone of voice.

Be strong.

Time to implement phase one of my plan to fool daddy's spies. Sucking in a quick breath, I whirled to see Auric looking as gorgeous as I remembered, but instead of saying hi, I just gave him a cool smile and went around him to take up my spot behind the bar.

The jerk, of course, acted just as aloof and followed his buddies—another thing to peeve me off; he hadn't come alone—to a table in the back. He then signaled for Trixie, tonight's waitress, to serve them.

Seriously?

Two could play at this game. I ignored him hard, refusing to look over at his table, but meanwhile making sure I posed at my best. Leaning low over the bar to wipe it down. Flinging my hair whenever I bent down to grab something. Hell, I even climbed my three-step stool and shook my ass while scrubbing the mirror behind the bar, which hadn't been cleaned since my last temper tantrum.

But the jerk stayed at his table. And yes I knew what he was doing—or in this case not doing—despite my determination to not peek, I couldn't help myself. I glanced his way a few times to gauge his reaction, yet while I noticed his companions seemed to be watching me with interest, Auric didn't seem to be looking at me at all.

Fuming—and astonished—I handed the bar over to Frank, my Friday night muscle, and flounced off to my office in the back to work on the accounts —AKA pout.

How could I have been so wrong about him? He'd kissed me. And liked it. He'd come to the bar. But not alone.

What kind of game was he playing? And how could I cheat?

When the knock sounded, I assumed it was Trixie with another boyfriend problem. You'd think a tree would spread her leaves around, but she really had the hots for a topiary on some rich dude's property in the west end.

I shouted out "come in" while still chewing the stub of my pencil. Math and I did not get along, as proven by the numbers in front of me that refused to add up. A computer might have helped, but my last two had been infested with gremlins and I'd yet to buy a third.

The sharp scent of cologne and leather permeated my space and invaded my senses. Startled, I glanced up to see Auric smiling enigmatically at me. He shut the door, locked it, and leaned against it.

My beating heart sped up.

"Nice office," he said.

Nicer since he'd arrived. Smaller, too. "What do you want?" I said, more sharply than intended. I was still miffed he'd ignored me earlier, never mind that I'd started it.

"When can you leave?" he asked, ignoring my question.

"Anytime, since there's a full staff tonight. Why?" I answered without thinking. His very masculine presence in the confines of my office seemed to be doing weird things to my mental state and libido. Kind of like a sexual stimulant that had the hormones in my body hopping up and down screaming, "Take me."

"Good. You're taking the rest of the night off. We're going to dinner now." He said this as if there was no doubt as to my answer.

"We are?" I thought about questioning his caveman tactics but, to be honest, talk about a turn-on. Me man, you woman. Feminists be damned—actually, they already had been. They now burned their bras in Hell, to my father's eternal headache. Needless to say, curiosity made me decide to see where Auric was going with this.

Only one problem: we couldn't leave via the front or my dad's spies would spot us and rat us out. Call me chicken, but I wasn't quite ready for Auric to meet my dad yet.

"Follow me and we'll sneak out the side door." I wasn't usually one to play hooky so the sheer audacity of it would please my father to no end. Wait a second. I couldn't tell dad I was shirking work to be with Auric. Bummer. Here I was, a perfectly sinful daughter and I couldn't even reap the reward.

"Why sneak?"

Quick, lie. "Because if we don't, my father will ground me for an eternity, and you might end up in several pieces." Or tell the truth because he'd never believe it.

"Overprotective?"

"You have no idea," I muttered. I quickly grabbed my jacket and purse before I led him to the exit that opened onto the alley. Pushing on the metal bar, the door squeaked as it opened. I stuck my head out and looked both ways to ensure we didn't have any tattlers lurking outside.

"Are you that ashamed of being seen with me?" Auric arched a brow at my antics.

"Trust me. It's better this way." Way better, especially if he remained in possession of his body parts.

Shrugging, he followed me out into the alley. Seeing no one around, I breathed an inaudible sigh of relief. I didn't speak until we'd made it to the street behind the club and started walking away.

"Going to explain what that was all about?" Asked as his hand casually reached for mine again.

His simple touch made the temperature in my body go up a notch—make that several.

I quickly squelched my tingle of pleasure at this act. He probably did that with all the girls he walked with. A thought that made me see red. The bloody kind as I—

Stow the murderous impulse. Auric was with me. No need to kill anyone. Yet. The night was young.

But back to Auric and his question. Explain my actions. Um, no. "I'll take the fifth on that."

To my surprise, he didn't push the matter. Didn't ask me anything else at all as a matter of fact. The longer we walked in silence, the more nuts it drove me until I blurted out, "Can I ask what prompted the dinner invite?"

"So you can ask questions, but I can't?"

"Are you still pissy that I made you sneak out the back?"

He halted and forced me to face him. "I am not pissy."

"Grumpy."

"How about frustrated."

Before I could ask what frustrated him, he showed me.

Hard lips swooped against mine, a bruising kiss that slammed into me with the force of a hurricane.

And that was stopped too soon.

I made a noise. "Get back over here."

"Why were you ignoring me?" he shot back instead. "Is this about last night? About me leaving when David came looking for me?"

Blame him. Put him on a guilt trip. Make him apologize.

All sound advice taught to me over the years, but valid only if I wanted to manipulate. I didn't want to string Auric along like a puppet. I wanted something different with him. Something real. Honest. "I was told to stay away from you."

Auric didn't register any shock. On the contrary, a hint of a smile curved his lips. "You're not doing a very good job."

"What can I say? I'm a bad girl."

"Or a very good one," he teased, his hand cupping my waist and drawing me forward, pressing me against his hardness.

There was no way I could stem the arousal consuming me. What was it about Auric that affected me so? And dammit, as I found myself staring at his face, I wondered why he had to be so bloody attractive. His scar should have detracted from his beauty, but instead, it enhanced it. It gave him a bolder, more sensual, and yet dangerous look that excited my hormones to no end.

"Who told you to stay away me?" he asked. "Your sister Bambi?"

Tell him that Lucifer, father of all sin and the girl he'd just kissed, had a hate on for him? Maybe too soon. I shook my head. "It doesn't matter who said what. I make my own choices."

"Sure you do; that's why you were ignoring me and we sneaked out the side door like a dirty secret. I won't be played."

Then he was dating the wrong girl. "I wasn't ignoring you. I was playing hard to get. When you said you would see me, I assumed alone. Then you showed up with your buddies and..."

"You got mad."

"Yes."

"Are you still mad?"

My turn to brush a light kiss on his lips and dance out of reach when he would have taken more. "All is forgiven."

My answer seemed to satisfy him, and we resumed walking, his thumb lazily stroking my hand. This simple act had my libido in a heightened state of awareness, something I kept trying to tamp down.

"Not the talkative type, are you?" I said after we'd walked another block in silence. "I don't suppose you'd like to tell me where we're going?"

"Shh," he said, putting a callused finger against my lip.

I thought about biting his finger—and then licking it. A plan I abstained from when I saw him watching the dark around us intently.

Blame him for distracting me from safety rule number one. Always be aware of your surroundings. I'd had enough attempts on my life to know better than to let my guard down. Not to mention there still existed the possibility that one of Dad's minions had caught our trail and followed us. That was all I needed, Dad barging in on a romantic dinner.

At least, I assumed Auric meant for this to be romantic. He hadn't really explained why he wanted dinner with me. Given he seemed fairly human, I was going to assume he wasn't a cannibal and thinking of having me for dinner.

Who cared about who ate who. Back to the reality at hand. Possible danger.

I tuned my enhanced senses to the night around us and detected...nothing. So I gave in to impulse and licked the finger that still rested against my lips.

Vivid green eyes turned to face me, and I grinned impishly before nipping his finger.

"Ow!" Auric pulled his offended digit away and scowled at me.

I smiled wider. "Don't ever shush me," I said.

"Did it ever occur to you that maybe I was doing it for your own safety?"

"And did it ever occur to you that I'm a big girl who can take care of herself?" The irony of it all, though, was I loved it when a guy got all medieval and protective. I just wished my feminist side would allow me to enjoy it without the snark.

"We're here," he said, in a change of subject.

The warehouse-type building in front of us seemed rather ordinary, and was it me or was there nary a sign of a restaurant to be seen?

"Is it a secret dining establishment?"

"No, it's called my kitchen," he said, unlocking a heavy-duty steel door.

"You cook?" I couldn't help the high questioning note as I followed him through the door and up a wide set of stairs.

"Very well, actually," was the reply he tossed over his shoulder.

At this point, I shut up and tried to enjoy the view—or I would have if his damn leather duster hadn't been in the way. I wondered if he'd object to taking it off before walking up the rest of the stairs. Deciding this request would be too forward, even for me, I pondered, instead, the fact that he'd invited me to dinner in his apartment.

Now, most girls right about now would be thinking, "Wait a second, I barely know this guy. He could be a psycho. What if he has nefarious plans?" But I'm not most girls. And I had a sneaky feeling Auric wasn't most guys.

Besides, most important of all, and fun, Dad would have a kitten if he knew I was here.

Three flights of stairs later, which left neither of us breathing hard—confirming my belief he wasn't just pretty muscle—he unlocked another riveted steel door and we entered his lair.

As man caves went, his proved rather disappointing. No red velvet. No chains hanging from the ceiling. No dim lighting or soft music playing. Instead, I walked into a cavernous space. Being a converted warehouse, the ceiling stretched way above me and had iron beams and piping running throughout, along with lighting suspended on steel wires. Tinted windows made up one wall, with a half-decent view of the city.

In one corner, he had some heavy-duty exercise

equipment: punching bag, treadmill, weights, and various other contraptions of torture. The center of the room seemed to be a living-slash-dining area with an L-shaped leather couch facing a big screen television and, behind the couch area, a rather boring wooden kitchen table and four chairs.

The back wall had his kitchen area, with gleaming black cabinets and a granite countertop, along with some serious stainless steel appliances, complete with an island and stools. Turned out he might have been serious when he said he could cook.

Glancing away from his kitchen, I looked over the rest of his place. The back end of his loft had been partially closed in and had two doors. More than likely a bathroom and storage.

In the final corner of his abode, and this was where I perked up, he had one massive, I mean we're talking gi-normous, bed. A four poster, wooden beast, piled high with pillows. Now there was a bed made for sinning.

"We can test it later, if you'd like," he whispered in my ear, his hot breath making my knees go weak and my panties wet.

But I'd been propositioned before. "Sorry, but I'm holding out for love," I said before plopping my ass on one his stools.

Dead silence. Why was it, whenever I mentioned the L-word, men got tongue-tied?

"And how long before you decide it's love?" he asked. His lips pressed hotly against my neck. "One date." Kiss. "Two." Nibble.

"I don't know how long it takes. I've yet to fall in love. I'm beginning to wonder if I'll ever meet the right man to give myself to." Okay, I wasn't really wondering, but hoping. Hoping Auric was the one.

"Wait a second." Auric twirled the stool around so I faced him. "Are you, in your own special way, trying to tell me you're still a virgin?"

I could tell by the look on his face that he found this hard to believe.

"One hundred percent virgin."

"Bullshit."

Such shock. And yet it was the truth. "No lie. You are looking at a bona fide virgin. Intact cherry and all the rest. Although, it should be noted, that while I've yet to do the horizontal mambo, I've kissed and petted a bit. Even made it to second base once."

For a second his eyes went funny, and he opened his mouth twice as if to speak, but he swallowed hard instead. Without a word, he moved away from me to stand behind the island, his back to me. For a moment he stood still before he opened the fridge and pulled out some stuff.

His lack of comment intrigued me. In the past, whenever I announced my untouched state, I then became inundated with impassioned speeches from the guys I was dating about how they were *the one*. A few even made false declarations of love.

Unfortunately for them, my father hadn't raised a fool. I spotted their lies. Couldn't handle their faults. Didn't want them.

In the end, I dumped all my boyfriends before we got to the deed. Had I made a mistake? Hard to tell. I wasn't quite sure what love would look or feel like, but I somehow figured I'd know it when it finally hit me.

Watching Auric as he sliced, diced, and sautéed his way around the kitchen did strange things to me. My heart fluttered—and my pussy ached. My feelings for him were uncharted territory. Exciting new ground.

He's the one.

Such conviction, and yet, I still had to put Auric to the test. I needed to find out now, before I got any more involved, if a relationship between us could work. This meant a lot of honesty on my part, and I hoped his.

"Who taught you to cook?" I asked.

"I taught myself. It was that or starve. And you? Do you cook at all?"

"I'm better at cooking trouble," I retorted, an answer that he rewarded with a chuckle. Think chocolate that melted on your tongue, yanked forth a groan, and made your taste buds sing. Yeah, that was what that low sound of his did to me. He spoke or laughed, and just about each time, it sent a shiver through my body and made my nipples take notice.

Not one to waste an opportunity, I shrugged off my jacket and let my beamers do their trick.

It took him a second to notice, but when he did, and cut himself, I inwardly grinned. I might not be a true succubus, but I knew how to get a man's attention.

We chatted about inane things while he cooked —and I behaved. When the smells became mouthwatering, he finally scooped his masterpiece onto plates and carried them over to his dented wooden table. I dug in and groaned in pleasure.

Sautéed chicken, mushrooms, onions, some veggies, and angel hair pasta. The man was a god of the kitchen.

"Oh, I hope you're a chef in real life because you'd be wasted doing anything else." Tummy full, and stretching my yoga pants, I wondered if I dared lick the plate clean. This wasn't dinner at home, so I abstained and, instead, leaned back to sip at the wine he'd served us.

"Cooking is a hobby of mine."

"So what do you do for work?"

"This and that," was his vague reply.

A frown creased my forehead. "That's not an answer."

"I'm not at liberty to say, or I would." He shrugged. "Besides, who cares about my job? I'm more interested in you."

I admit, while I found his air of mystery exciting, it also bothered me. Did he have something to hide, or did he mean what he said about wanting to know more about me? "Let me ask you something first. Is this a date?"

Auric's brows lifted. "What else would it be? We're in my apartment, eating a home-cooked meal with dim lighting. I'm a man, and you're a gorgeous woman." He smiled wickedly. "Where I come from, we call that a date."

I almost blushed. How hilarious, and unlike me. "Oh, in that case then, what do you want to know about me?"

"You're not one to mince words, are you?"

"Nope."

Auric chuckled. "Just who are you, Muriel, virgin and hellhound banisher?"

Having made the decision to test him, I gave him a quick and honest rundown. "I'm twenty-three and a Libra. I have a half-brother who is slated to possibly end the world, and quite a few sisters." Now there was an understatement. My dad wasn't shy about spreading his lust. "I live alone. No pets. Although, I do like dogs. I like to read corny romances. Watch adventure movies. Love fast food and pizza, hate seafood. Hmm, what else? Oh, my favorite color is pink, and my father is Satan."

CHAPTER TEN

I KNEW IT WAS PROBABLY TOO SOON TO TELL HIM that part, but considering how he made me feel and judging by his lack of panic at the appearance of hell-hounds, I figured he should know. After all, if Dad ever found out about our little romantic dinner, it wasn't inconceivable that he might pay Auric a visit.

Apparently Auric paid attention because he choked on his wine. "I'm sorry," he said, gasping and laughing at the same time. "I think I misunderstood the last part."

"What, that my favorite color is pink?" I said, being deliberately obtuse.

"No, the part after that."

"Oh, that I'm Satan's daughter." I declared this proudly. I usually hid my identity for safety reasons, not out of shame.

"You're not serious, are you?" His brows drew together, almost close enough to touch.

"Yes, I'm serious. My name is Satana Muriel Baphomet. But I like to go by Muriel. My dad is Lucifer, Lord of All Sin, punisher of the damned. As for the other half of my gene pool, I have no idea; but from what I've gleaned over the years, she wasn't a hundred-percent mortal. Is this going to be a problem?" I held my breath as I waited for a reply. His answer here would make or break this fragile relationship we'd forged. I could change a lot of things about myself, except my family; they were forever.

"I don't believe this," he muttered. "You can't be a princess of Hell."

"Why not?"

"Because," he sputtered, "you're cute."

"What did you expect? A hag?"

"Someone more demonic at least."

"Bambi doesn't look like a demon."

"She's a succubus. She's supposed to be a sexy temptation.

"Aha!" I said, latching onto that instead of his difficulty in accepting my parentage. "You did notice she was hot."

"Of course I did. Anything with a dick would have noticed her, but I still thought you were cuter."

"You did?"

"I did. But now..." He scrubbed his face. "I can't believe you're the spawn of the devil."

"Believe it, but also know that just because he's my father doesn't make me evil."

"What does that make you then? Are you going to try and make me believe that you're a force for good?"

"Why must everything be in terms of good or evil? Why can't I just be me?" I exclaimed. "I'm not perfect. I sometimes forget my manners. Or take my uncle's name in vain. Every now and then, I kill something. But I don't kill wantonly, only those threatening me or those I love. And I do love; my dad, my sisters, even my annoying brother. All I want is for someone to like me, for me. Not because they want to curry favor with my father, not because they want to get close to kill me."

"Then why tell anyone who your dad is? Why not keep it a secret?"

"Because I'm not ashamed of my dad. I'm not ashamed of me. And if I'm thinking of getting serious with a guy, then he should know the truth before things go any further." It looked as if it had been a good idea to get this out in the open now, instead of later. Auric had reacted much as I feared he would.

"And just where do you think this is going, Muriel, *daughter of Satan?*"

I didn't like his tone. "Screw you. To think I was beginning to think you might be the one. It's why I agreed to come to dinner with you. I should have known better."

Annoyed at his reaction to a parentage I had no control over, I got up and snagged my jacket as I stalked for the door. I didn't get far. An iron grip on my arm stopped me.

"Where do you think you're going?"

"Somewhere else."

"Why? I thought we were having a good time."

"Me, too, until you turned into a jerk." I felt no qualms about insulting him, not when inside I was practically crying. Would I ever find someone to accept who I was?

"Can't a guy have a moment to absorb a startling revelation? You can't just drop a bomb like that and expect me to just blink and go on." He slid his hands from my arms to settle loosely on my waist.

"Do you have any idea how hard it is to tell people who I am?" I hated the tears that pooled in my eyes. I didn't want his pity. "As soon as I tell people who my dad is, suddenly they can't run away fast enough or out come the crosses and knives."

"I haven't run," he said softly.

"Yet." I refused to allow myself to hope. Hope led to disappointment. Disappointment led to me complaining to Dad, which, in turn, led to him loosing some of his minions on the world in retaliation.

"I'm not going anywhere."

"Hard to kill me if I'm not in the same room," I sniffled.

"I am not going to kill you."

"I've heard that one before, too," I whispered before dropping my head.

"I'm sorry you've been hurt." He lifted a hand and brushed at the tears that clung to my lower lashes. I wanted to turn my cheek into that hand, but pride—and fear—stayed me.

"Pain has always been a part of my life. It comes with being who I am. And there's times I hate it." He was the first I'd ever admitted this to. Even Bambi never knew how the rejection and betrayal of those around me hurt.

How pathetic I sounded. Needy. Ugh. I wanted to slap myself. I also wanted to run away before I saw the pity on his face. I wanted to scream at the unfairness of it all. But most of all, I just wanted to be accepted.

So I stood trembling in front of him, waiting for him to join the ranks of those who'd hurt me in the past. I'd survived their rejection, and I would survive his—eventually.

A finger tilted my chin so I would look at him. "In spite of who you are, I like you, Muriel."

"And I like you." I also thought I was falling in love with him, not that those words would cross my lips.

"You'd better." He growled as he drew me closer to him.

I closed my eyes and waited. He brushed his lips across mine, feather-soft, but enough that an electric shock ran through me and then centered in my pelvis, causing erotic havoc. Strong arms came around me, and I reveled in his solid strength. My body brushed up against the hardness of his, and my hormones screamed in joy. I rejoiced even more that he hadn't pushed me away.

He tugged at my full lower lip, and I parted my mouth slightly to be rewarded with the feel of his tongue against my lips and teeth.

Testing my French knowledge, I opened my mouth wider and let my tongue come out to play, touching the tip of his with mine.

A burning jolt of desire ignited my body. I now

understood the term 'instant fireworks'. I wanted to shove him up against a wall and maul his body. Having a little restraint, though, I contented myself with feeling him up through his shirt, enjoying the feel of his firm muscles all over. I melted against his broad chest, a move rewarded with his arms wrapping tight around me, cocooning me in his strength. My hands traveled down his back, and I daringly rested my palms on his tight ass.

I squeezed.

If it hadn't been for the sound of tinkling glass, I was pretty sure he would have returned the groping favor. However, I doubted the sound of breaking windows on the third floor was a good sign. I knew this from experience, and no, I preferred not to go into details.

The timing of the attack sucked, though. Would I ever get to kiss Auric properly, without interruption?

Breaking off the kiss, we turned to face the jagged hole in the window—him sporting a half-crouched battle stance, me, an annoyed one.

At first I didn't see anything moving, and I briefly wondered if someone had just gotten lucky with a rock. Then I heard the sound of claws clicking over the hardwood floor. A familiar sound if you lived in hell, a really bad one to hear on this plane, for mortals at least. I wasn't too worried about myself. However, I still hadn't figured out what Auric was and what he was capable of.

Not knowing if he'd break easily, I decided on a course of safety. "Um, Auric, we might want to leave."

"Not fucking likely," he snapped, not taking his eyes off the couch behind which hid our visitor. Auric inched backwards toward the kitchen.

Rolling my eyes, I again had to question why men had to be so stubborn. "Seriously, Auric, you do not want to mess with this thing."

"I've dealt with demons before."

He had? When?

I'd have to ask later because my eyes widened and my jaw dropped as he pulled out a sword from behind his kitchen counter. I had to admit being impressed—his sword was long, shiny, and hard. Wait, that didn't sound right. Needless to say, he had a big one, and judging by the way he moved it, he also knew how to use it.

Damn, how was it possible I was even hornier than before?

Since I was done admiring his sword—unless he chose to drop his pants—I addressed what he'd said.

"What do you mean you've dealt with demons before?" My Auric had hidden depths to him, it seemed.

"Could we discuss this later? This isn't the time." He flashed me a quick look as he inched toward the couch and what lay crouched behind it.

Was he getting sassy with me? I could see why it annoyed my dad. Initially, I'd planned on taking care of the demon myself, but his arrogance annoyed me, so I decided to let whatever had made an appearance toy with Auric first, before I saved his ass.

I hopped onto a stool and crossed my legs to watch. Auric moved with a sinuous grace that I had to admire, and with his coat finally shed, I also got to ogle his fine ass as it moved in his tight jeans. Yummy.

When he got within a foot of the couch, the intruder pounced. A minor demon, I'd say, by the size of it. Lots of tooth, claw, and leathery wings, but no magic. I could have flattened it without breaking a nail, and I'd probably still have to if Auric turned out to be all look and talk with no walk.

Turned out he had a lot of walk. He swung his sword like an extension of himself, making it arc and swoop impossibly fast and fluent. I admit to being impressed. The little demon didn't stand a chance, especially once I realized the sword had been spelled. The blue glow and the burning sizzle whenever Auric struck the demon gave it away.

In no time at all, Auric had injured the demon enough that it lay prone on the floor, breathing heavily, black ichor leaking from numerous cuts, none of them deadly, but the sword point at its throat? Yeah, there was no coming back from that.

Instead of finishing him off, though, Auric asked it a question. "Why are you here?"

"To slay," hissed the ugly creature.

I rolled my eyes. Talk about obvious. I hopped off the stool and walked over to them. As I loomed over the minor demon, I checked it out, not recognizing it. Not that I knew every demon in Hell, but I knew a fair bit; some I even considered friends.

"Putrid hell whore," it spat.

"Watch your filthy mouth." Auric lifted his sword to strike the killing blow that would send it back to Hell, but I stayed his hand. Not out of any pity for the creature, but because I wanted an answer.

"Kill who?" I asked.

"Lucifer's daughter," it cackled.

I frowned at it. "I know who I am. I asked who you were told to kill."

"You."

"Me?" I squeaked. I wasn't scared, just annoyed at its effrontery. I mean, seriously, did he really think his not-so-impressive ass could have kicked mine? "That's ridiculous. My dad is going to rip out your innards when you get back to Hell, you little rodent." And I was tempted to follow and kick him around a few times, too, for breaking up one smoking-hot kiss.

Auric's voice rumbled, and he didn't sound happy. "Who wants Muriel dead?"

"The one who would rule Hell. My master, G—" The little demon began choking up gobs of black blood and bile.

Eeww!

Auric and I both stepped back—me mostly to save my boots—and watched the creature's body as it convulsed, its limbs thrashing hard against the floor. With a high-pitched squeal of pain, the demon's body caved in on itself, shrinking in size until, with a pint-sized scream, it winked out of sight, and, judging by the burst of energy at the end, permanently.

Not good. See, usually when a demon was vanquished on the mortal realm, it wasn't the end, more of a direct ticket back to Hell. Only in the pit could demons be killed and stay dead.

But this demon had just self-destructed. He'd not gotten sucked into a mini portal rip back to my home. He'd poofed right out of existence.

I'd never seen that happen before. "I've got to go." I had to tell my dad about this. Someone had managed to completely destroy a demon from afar, an act that should have been impossible.

"Given this attack was aimed at you, I think you should stay here. It's not safe for you out there. I don't mind you hanging out until we figure out what's going on." He said this while wiping down his sword blade with his napkin from dinner.

Stay? I looked at him in disbelief. Then snorted. "Nice try, Casanova, but the making-out thing is going to have to wait for another time. I've got to go talk to my dad and ask him what, by the hag's hairy tit, is going on."

"What are you talking about now?" Auric appeared confused. "This isn't a ploy to get in your pants."

"It's not?" How disappointing.

"You heard what the demon said. It was after you. You're in danger."

"Welcome to my life. Daughter of Satan, remember? This isn't the first time it's happened, and it probably won't be the last. My dad made sure I could protect myself at an early age. Speaking of which, some of my weapons are back at my place, so if there's going to be a bunch of demons gunning for me, then I need to get ready." Not to mention one of the first things Dad had done when I'd moved out on my own was ensure my apartment was portal- and demon-proof, well, except for him, of course. The only way demons could enter my place was through the door, and by invitation only.

"You're not going alone. I'm coming with you." Auric moved to a cabinet against the wall. When he opened it, I almost clapped my hands in glee, for my handsome suitor had almost as many cool toys as I did.

Swords, knives, guns, and, yes, even a flamethrower. I could feel another piece of my heart swinging in his direction, and I had to stifle an urge to throw my arms around him and kiss him silly.

I watched him slide silver knives into his boots in cleverly hidden sheaths and up his sleeves with leather straps. I shook my head in bemusement. Auric just seemed too perfect to be true. I'd have to find his major flaw soon.

Oh wait, he does have one; he likes me. He had to be slightly crazy to want to stick around now that he knew the truth.

The final touch to his deadly ensemble—his leather duster, of course. He swung it on, hiding his arsenal, and held his hand out to me, his eyes so vividly intense that I caught my breath.

As if in slow motion, I walked to him and put my hand in his; his warm strength made me feel alive and closer to someone than I'd ever felt. For a girl who'd spent most of her life alone, almost friendless, this contact seemed precious to me. Auric knew my deepest secret. He was starting to see some of the ugly parts of my life, and yet he hadn't run.

Yeah, but wait until he meets Dad, chortled my stupid inner voice.

Shut up, I snarled back.

I hated it when I was right.

CHAPTER ELEVEN

When we emerged from Auric's building, his friends were just walking up. I threw Auric a suspicious look. He shot me an enigmatic smile. I'd not seen him call anyone, and yet, there they were.

"Muriel, may I introduce my long-time companions, David and Christopher."

David smiled at me shyly while Christopher swept me a bow.

"Hi, nice to meet you." And it was. Auric had good looking, not to mention interesting, friends. "I have a brother named Christopher." Or as my father lamented, that good-for-nothing who refused to take his spot as his evil right hand in Hell.

I tried to not look offended when David sniffed around me and Auric. I hadn't showered in a few hours, but I had good deodorant. However, it wasn't our scent he was after. Being a shape shifter, I knew he had to have a keen sense of smell and excellent night vision. It seemed to be a species trait. His nose led him upwards where, we could all see the jagged glass left in the window.

"Did you get a visitor, by any chance?" David asked.

"Nothing I couldn't handle." Auric shrugged.

Again, I felt like rolling my eyes. I could have handled the little demon, too, a reminder that made me frown. If someone meant to kill me, why on earth would they send such a weakling to attack me first and give the whole jig away? Anybody who knew me would have known it would take something a lot bigger than that.

Something about this didn't make sense, making me more determined than ever to get home and call Dad. I had a special phone line to Hell, my father's way of making sure I kept in touch, not that I needed to use it often, with his almost daily impromptu visits. Someone still had a hard time letting go.

Back to the situation at hand, I realized something else. Auric's friends didn't seem to be shocked about the fact that a demon had attacked. Just who were these mysterious hunks?

Christopher, the wizard who looked nothing like

my brother, didn't look happy, and he frowned at Auric. "The magical wards I put on your place should have prevented demonic entry."

I sheepishly put up my hand and waved it. "Guilty." When Christopher looked at me questioningly, I explained. "I'm like a walking no-magic zone. Spells don't work around me; I probably deactivated your wards when I entered his place. Sorry."

"But you didn't affect my sword," said Auric, placing his hand on the hilt.

So many dirty things I could have said at the point—the main one being, *Let me touch your sword and see what happens.* I didn't mean the metal one, in case that wasn't clear.

"Your sword is blessed, right?" I asked on a hunch.

"Yes. Does that make a difference?"

"I'm Satan's daughter; of course it does. Your sword is imbued with holy magic. I can't negate it. It, along with a few others, aren't affected by my power."

Too late, I realized that perhaps I shouldn't have said that last bit out loud; maybe the first bit as well, judging by the saucer-sized eyes on David and Christopher. To tell the truth, I figured Auric would tell them at some point anyway. But telling them about my weak spot, mainly blessed items, that was just dumb. After all, I didn't really know these guys, and here I'd just given them an important clue if they ever decided to get rid of me instead of date me.

My dad always said I talked before thinking. Oh, well, the damage had been done. I'd pretend I didn't say it and hope they didn't mean me ill.

Auric's arm curved around my waist, a masculine gesture I quite enjoyed, and he squeezed me as if to reassure me. We walked toward my place as he filled his friends in quietly about the demon.

Surprisingly enough, his friends didn't question me about the whole being-related-to-the-devil thing, which I appreciated since I found myself busy basking in the feeling of being so close to Auric. Not to mention how distracted he kept me with his fingers lightly stroking the skin of my waist. I'd have to remember to always wear short tops around him.

"How is it you live so close to the bar and me, yet I've never run into any of you guys before?"

"We were busy," was Auric's short reply. His friends were even worse at the nonchalance game, judging by their pretended interest in the night sky.

"Busy doing what?" I narrowed my gaze. Evasion was a game I knew.

So did he. And he cheated. Instead of answering,

Auric drew me up on my tiptoes and kissed me soundly. When he relinquished my mouth, I found myself breathless and flushed. But I hadn't missed the fact that he'd avoided my question once again.

A mystery. It annoyed and thrilled me at the same time. I'd told him my dirty, awful secrets, well, some of them anyway. He owed me the same in return if he wanted to put those luscious lips on mine again. Wait, he just had. Damn.

I didn't know if I liked the fact that his kisses distracted me, but I did know it irritated me that he'd noticed and used it against me. Not that I would protest overly much. What could I say? The man kissed like a god. The term 'mind-blowing' came to mind. I wondered if this erotic effect he had over me would wear off over time. I'd have to kiss him some more and find out. Sigh, the things I had to do. At least this was a hard task I looked forward to.

As we came into sight of my building, the shadows spread even more deeply between the buildings and parked cars. No surprise, the street-light was burnt out yet again.

The men slowed down and formed a protective wall in front of me that was utterly adorable. I was about to goose them for fun when a shadowy figure detached itself from the wall and moved toward us.

I heard the scrape of metal as Auric drew his sword and noted David had untucked his shirt while Christopher pulled forth his expanding staff—the wooden one, perverts!

What had them spooked? Standing on tiptoe, I craned to peek over three sets of broad shoulders, but they formed an effective barrier. So I walked around them to greet the oncoming figure.

From behind me, I heard the mutter of ancient words that vibrated in the air and the scuff of a step as someone took a step forward, probably Auric, to flank me. I raised a hand to wave them back. "Calm down. It's okay. I know the guy. He's a friend." I turned to the cloaked figure. "Charon, what are you doing here? Is everything all right at the bar?"

"Your father sent me. We must speak." The hooded visage looked past me to my companions. "Alone."

Anxiety brewed in my belly. Charon had never come to my place before, and the fact that he did so with a message from my dad did not bode well. It also didn't help that he'd caught me with not one but all three of the guys I was supposed to avoid.

Oops. In my frazzle—the one caused by the kisses and not the demon—I'd forgotten.

Here was to hoping Charon forgot to tell my dad,

too. "Thanks for dinner," I said as I turned and pasted a smile on my face, a false smile of reassurance that I knew didn't reach my eyes. "Maybe we could do it again sometime."

Not entirely untrue. Now to see if I'd ever get the chance. I whirled away from the guys and had started walking to the front door of my building, Charon close by my side, when I sensed a presence on my other side. Not entirely surprised, I glanced over to see Auric, a stubborn smirk on his face.

"You're not ridding yourself of me that easily. As a matter of fact, I am not going anywhere until I know that you're safe." Did he have to sound so hot when he pulled the whole macho-protector routine?

Wasn't he just the cutest? But still. "I'm safe with Charon, and I can take care of myself."

"That's not the point. You shouldn't have to."

Surely that wasn't a tear in my eye over the sweetest thing anyone ever said to me. It deserved a reply. "Don't think acting all caveman-like is getting you in my panties."

Some guys would have said something cocky at this point. Auric just doused me with that lethal smile of his, which made me fume and smile in equal parts.

Reaching the condo ahead of us, he held open

the door for Charon and me to walk in. Had I not been so bemused, I would have noticed the door was unlocked and probably sensed the creature that lay in wait, but Auric had my hormones in a frenzy. Before I knew it, the creature managed to tangle its claws in my hair and yank me sideways. I heard Auric bellow something, but being somewhat busy trying not to be scalped, I had no idea what he said.

Anyone who has had their hair pulled knows the pain. It was like every freaking strand singing a high-pitched soprano. Did I mention I wasn't crazy about opera? And when I'm in pain, I get mad. Really mad.

Still wearing my kick-ass boots, I stomped my heel down on the foot, more like clodhopper tipped in claws, of the thing that held me. Even as it keened in pain, the sharp stiletto of my heel scoring deep, my elbow jabbed back, hard, into the creature's ribs. This had the effect of loosening the hold in my hair, allowing me to twist away.

In one smooth motion, I pivoted around, hands upraised. Words of a spell suddenly flooded my mind, and I spit them out. I never knew where or how this knowledge came to me, only that when I spoke these powerful words, magic happened. Magic struck. Magic annihilated. The accosting demon didn't have time to scream or even writhe; it simply ceased to be.

Poof. Gone. Fuck.

I stared at the sifting black dust in shock. Since when could I utterly destroy a demon with my magic? In the past, when in need, my innate magic allowed me to banish demons or place a stasis hold on them until bigger help arrived. This complete destruction floored me. Where had this spell come from? And... Why now? What was happening? Yet another reason I needed to speak to my father.

Danger taken care of, I schooled my features so as to not let my companions know how much my destruction of the demon bothered me. I finger combed my hair and turned with a bright smile to Auric and Charon. "Where were we? Ah, yes, I was trying to explain to Auric that I could take care of myself." To my intense pleasure, he gave me a grudging nod of acknowledgement, but he still refused to budge.

"I never doubted you could take care of yourself; I'd just feel better if you didn't have to do it alone."

I closed my mouth; what could I say? In the space of only minutes, he'd said the second most sweetest thing evah! If I wasn't planning to kiss him before, I was planning to now—and in a much more interesting spot than his lips.

In a gesture of trust to my abilities, he let me go up the stairs first, with Charon between us. Auric brought up the rear, and a perverse part of me hoped he was checking out my ass. I gave my booty an extra wiggle, just in case.

When we got to my apartment, Auric took the key from my hand and went in first. I could feel Charon beside me, shaking in silent mirth. He'd known me too long. I nudged him and whispered, "I think it's cute, so can it. I've never had anyone want to protect me before."

"I know," Charon whispered. "It's just...does he know who you are and what you can do?"

"He knows who I am; as for what I can do, I don't even know myself sometimes."

"All clear," Auric called from inside.

Charon and I entered my small apartment, even smaller now that Auric loomed in it. I was suddenly glad I'd tidied up the place today before going to work. I'd hate for him to think I couldn't cook, and sucked as a housekeeper, even if it happened to be the truth. I had other skills. Although somehow 'killing demons' wasn't exactly a box a girl could check off on dating site questionnaires.

"Can I offer you guys something to drink?" I asked. I didn't wait for an answer as I took off my coat and threw it on a chair before walking into my tiny kitchen. I opened the fridge and grabbed a couple of cold beers—recent events called for alcoholic sustenance. In the drawer with the bottle opener, I eyed an array of emergency tools—I kept them stashed all over the place as a 'just in case'.

True killers and survivalists planned ahead. I palmed my silver needles—deadly and decorative—and used them to fix my hair up into a loose bun on top of my head. Contrary to popular films, long hair flinging about in a fight was never a good idea. Or had we so soon forgotten the hair pull in the lobby?

I carried the beers out to my guests. Auric stood at one end of my living room while Charon... I didn't know what to call what Charon did, but he did so from the other side.

Raising my bottle, I said, "Cheers." Then downed a good portion of mine. I left the guys swigging theirs as I wandered into my bedroom. I felt a need to arm myself with a few more toys.

Opening the hidden compartment in my headboard—custom-made of course—I pulled out my braided unicorn hair whip and placed it on the nightstand. It burned demons and other nasties better than holy water. It also reassured me that, while I might be a lot of things, demon wasn't one of them—the whip didn't hurt me. I also added a few more daggers about my person. I might have magic, but only an idiot went out armed with only one weapon.

Coming back out to my living room, I found Auric and Charon staring at each other; at least, I assumed Charon was staring. It was hard to tell with his hood and all.

I flopped into my chair and took another swallow of my beer before talking. "Okay, Charon, spill."

Charon jerked his hood at Auric.

Arms crossed over a wide chest. "I'm not leaving, so say what you need to Muriel." Auric looked like an immovable wall—and a stubborn ass. Both traits I happened to admire, as I held an abundance of those qualities myself.

"It's okay, Charon; I'm pretty sure he can be trusted. And if not, I can always kill him."

Auric looked offended by my remark, but hey, I'd only known him all of, like, three days. He hadn't had time to earn my full trust—or my heart—yet.

"Or feed him to the Styxx. The monsters love fresh meat."

"How about I give my word to keep what's said to myself?"

I snorted. "As if you wouldn't tell your friends. Don't make any promises. Then, that way, you don't have to break them." Although rule breaking might endear him to my dad.

"Is he the fellow your father was ranting about?" Charon asked.

"Your dad is the one who forbid you from seeing me?"

Caught. I bluffed my way out. "I'd say that isn't the important thing right now."

Charon tilted his head. "And yet the strands of fate are weaving furiously. You stand upon a cross-road, Lucifer's daughter. Which path shall you take?"

"How about the let's not turn all portent and preachy and get to why you're actually here in the middle of the night?" Because Charon was the type who liked to start work early and finish late, which made no sense, but that was Charon.

"Have you heard about the movement to overthrow Lucifer?" asked Charon.

"When isn't there a movement to overthrow him?" Seriously, it had been happening since the beginning of time, or so I'd been told.

"Well, this time, whoever is attempting it has managed to pull together some real muscle."

"So Dad will throw his legion at this little army and crush it."

"Except part of his legion is missing. And now he suspects those who are left."

"Who is behind the defections?" And why hadn't my father told me? If I'd known there was trouble, I'd have gone home to help out, even if the whole dutiful-daughter thing pissed him off. The fact that I'd be killing in his name would make up for it. With a last name like Baphomet, reputation was key. "Do we have a name? An address?" Heck, just give me a general direction. I'd ferret out the traitor.

Charon shook his hood. "That's just it. We don't know who is behind the rebellion."

"Are you even sure there is one?" It wouldn't be the first time Daddy got carried away by paranoia.

"The defecting demons that have been attacking some of your father's key supporters"— because even the devil needed allies—"aren't the only things missing. Damned souls have also been misplaced. And things are happening. Magical things that shouldn't be happening."

I knew of an example. "Like demons being blown up remotely."

"That and more. The thing is, the acts that have

been brought to your father's attention should be impossible. At least for anyone but your father."

"Could my uncle be behind it?"

Auric shifted his weight. "Your uncle?"

I shot him a quick glance. "Uncle God. He and my dad are constantly feuding. But this seems too underhanded for him."

"Indeed, Yahweh prefers open battlefields to this type of subtle attack. And we know of no one else truly capable. Your father has always been very careful to keep an eye on the other deities who might think to usurp his position."

A whole pantheon of gods made their home in the pit. Greek ones, like Zeus and Ares, Viking beings, such as Loki. Practically every deity ever worshipped now lived in the Pit. My uncle wasn't very good at opening his pearly gates to outsiders.

"Why are you here telling Muriel this?" Auric asked. "Why did her father not come himself?"

"Yeah, since when are you dad's messenger bitch?" And I wasn't being rude. There was a hell-hound trained for that task.

"He would have come himself, except, well..." Ever seen a hooded force to be reckoned with fidget instead of telling me why my dad wasn't here?

I glared. "Charon."

"Now don't get upset."

"*Charon.*" I practically growled his name this time. Was that smoke curling from my nose?

"Your dad was in an incident that temporarily incapacitated him."

I jumped from the chair. "What?"

"Your father's okay," Charon hastened to assure me. "Nothing that won't grow back, but given he's a little busy now hunting down the perpetrators and raising some Hell, he asked me to come check and warn you. He wanted to send a guard or two, but he knows how much you hate that. To be honest, they kind of have their hands busy right now."

"I should go to him." Daddy needed me.

"No!" Charon almost shouted; unusual for this usually mild mannered man—er, thing, or whatever Charon hid beneath the robe. "Your father wanted you to promise that you wouldn't go to Hell. Promise me, Muriel."

"I will not."

Charon stood taller...and taller until his head practically touched the ceiling. "Promise me. Or else."

Unlike my dad, I didn't ask what the 'or else' was. Charon was that spooky.

"Fine. I won't go to him." My words were very

specific because vows were very specific. I slouched back down into my chair, sulking. And I wasn't quiet about it. "When is Dad going to stop treating me like a little girl?"

Both Charon and Auric replied, "Never."

"So if I'm not allowed to go and play with Daddy, then what am I supposed to do instead?"

"Stay safe. Your father will come speak to you as soon as he can. Oh, and he had another message for you that didn't make much sense."

"What was it?"

"He said you were so grounded."

I laughed. When Auric looked at me, puzzled, and Charon cocked his head, I howled even harder until my eyes watered and I was gasping for air.

"I don't suppose you'll share with us what's so funny?" asked Auric.

I tried to stifle my laughter, not an easy task. I'd always had an odd sense of humor. "Remember how I told you I'd been forbidden to see you?"

"Yes," said Auric. Then I laughed again, as his face went slack with understanding. "Your dad threatened to ground you if you saw me?"

"Yup."

"And you disobeyed him?"

I winked. "Totally." Just like I would totally do it again. Auric tempted me that much.

With a shake of his head and a muttered, "Kids, they just never listen," Charon sketched a portal. Through the interdimensional slit, I could smell the brimstone of home and see the light of ash that fluttered through the crack. "Well, now that I've passed on the message, and you seem to be in good hands, I'll be off now. I'm sure my son's managed to do something stupid to the boat by now, and I have a feeling it's going to be busy at the river in the next little bit. Stay safe, Muriel. I'd rather not see your soul at the dock waiting for a ride."

How nice. He thought I had a soul. "Bye, Charon." I waved as he stepped through his rift. With a slight sucking of air, the portal disappeared.

"Well, I can certainly say there's never a dull moment around you," mused Auric aloud.

"It's all part of my charm," I said with a bright smile.

"So Satan warned you about me, did he?"

"I assume he meant you since he never actually used your name. Just 'that man.' He told me to stay away from you, or else."

"Or else what?" asked Auric, frowning. "What

does he mean by you're grounded? He's not going to bury you alive or something is he?"

I snorted. "Oh, please. Daddy would never actually hurt me. Maybe lock me up for a while, but I'd eventually escape. I am not a little girl anymore, and my dad can't tell me who I can date. So if you're worried about it, don't be. And if by chance he should show up and threaten you, let me know." Daddy might bear the title of King of Hell, but that didn't mean I would allow him to ruin this for me. I could do that all on my own.

"Speaking of showing up, shouldn't we be preparing this place a bit more, in case more demons come calling?"

"My place is safe. No demons in or out unless I invite them through that door. Well, except for Dad; you can't keep him out of anywhere."

"Why all the hardware, then?" he asked as he took in my shiny new accessories.

"I want to be prepared in case I need to leave quickly. Speaking of leaving, are you still determined to stay?"

"I'm not going anywhere, Muriel," said with a steady stare.

His words gave me an erotic thrill. Sure, I knew he meant tonight, but for a moment, I allowed myself to fantasize that he meant forever. "So, does your bar have the same magical shield as this place?"

"No. And how did you guess the bar was mine?"

"Please," he said with a roll of his eyes. "The way the staff defer to you, the office out back, the fact that you open it and lock up each night. And let's not forget the biggest clue, the fact that you're a walking no-magic field. Doesn't take a genius to figure it out."

"Oh." I added observant to his list of qualities. "You were asking about magical defenses for my bar. Given the nature of my clientele, I couldn't disallow portals or demons inside. They're great tippers when they get drunk. Of course, you have to make sure they don't steal the waitresses, but other than that, they're actually well behaved, especially compared to some other species."

"I get the impression the bar is your baby. I take it Daddy"—Auric almost choked when he called Satan 'Daddy', which made me smile—"didn't have a hand in it?"

"Nope, Nexus is all mine; and by this time next year, I hope to have a flat screen and a karaoke machine."

"Karaoke?" Auric laughed.

I tapped my foot and glared. "What's so funny about having karaoke? I happen to love it."

"Sorry." Auric tried to stifle his chuckles. Failed. "It's just the thought of some of your patrons singing. Well, let's just say I'd almost pay to see it."

I wanted to scowl some more, but he had a point. Didn't matter. I wanted karaoke in my bar, and dammit, I'd get it.

Auric moved closer to me, and it occurred to me we were alone again, and that made the kisses from earlier flare up in my mind.

Is it me or is it getting hot in here? My skin certainly flushed while another part of me moistened in preparation.

Oh no we aren't.

I had to get away from Auric before I did something foolish—or erotically interesting. "You know, you don't have to stay. I'll be perfectly fine here."

His reply? He flopped onto my couch and made himself comfortable.

I sighed as I turned away and headed for my linen closet. "I guess I'm grabbing you a blanket and pillow."

The chuckle from behind me sent shivers down my spine, the good kind.

I whipped around and found myself facing his very broad chest, a chest I was tempted to touch. I looked up and saw him smiling at me crookedly, with a mischievous twinkle in his eye. "Why are you following me?"

"I can't exactly protect you if I'm not in the same room as you."

"I told you we're safe here." Given his intent expression, I couldn't help but retreat, as well as lick lips that suddenly went dry.

"Put my faith in magic? No, thank you. What if you're wrong and something gets through? The time it takes for me to get to you could be deadly. Nope, I sleep where you sleep."

I wanted to stamp my foot in frustration. "We are not sharing a bed. I told you before I am not giving up my virginity until I find true love." Which was probably standing right in front of me, but I wanted to be sure.

"Who said anything about sex?" His eyes widened in false innocence. "I just said I needed to be in the same room as you."

"I–Um." I shut up. Stupid man. He'd flustered me again.

Hey, does that mean he doesn't want to have sex with me? "Wait a second. You don't find me attractive?"

"I didn't say that," he chided before tilting my chin. He kissed me lightly. Just one brief, butterfly touch before he moved away. "I want you. But I'll respect your wishes. I won't have intercourse with you. Unless you beg me to." The wise man uttered his tease and stepped out of reach.

Smart move because my fist had already begun to swing. He grabbed my clenched hand with a chuckle and pulled me up against his hard body. My body flushed with heat, especially when I remembered some of the fantasies I'd masturbated to the night before. I now knew first-hand my imagination hadn't done justice to what it would feel like to be pressed up against the length of his solid body.

The erotic pleasure that engulfed me at this simple touch frightened me, but even more, it excited me.

His arm curled around my waist and lifted me up so our lips were even. "You know," he whispered, his warm breath making me shiver with desire, "there are things we could do that would still leave you a virgin."

Surely the moan I heard didn't come from me? My mind and body were intrigued at his words. True, he had a point; but the thing I feared was, in the heat of the moment, I'd forgo my vow and indulge in pleasure for the sake of lust.

And would that be so bad? wondered my horny inner voice.

I would have loved to retort, both to him and myself, but my nose suddenly twitched. Was it me, or did I smell something familiar, something that was pounding on my door?

"Demon." An unnecessary statement, seeing as how Auric had already let go of me and turned, placing his body in front of mine as a shield. A second later, he unsheathed his sword—not the one I'd felt pressing against my lower belly, unfortunately.

I found his protectiveness cute, but he seemed to have missed one key point. "Um, Auric, whoever is banging isn't in the apartment."

Auric growled in reply. Seriously hot. But also not answering the door.

I walked around his bristling body and went to the vibrating panel. Flinging it open, I was very careful to stand back from the threshold. I knew the boundaries of the magic guarding my place.

A familiar chuckle made me groan and then let out a weary sigh as a demon I unfortunately knew loomed only inches from my doorway. "Hello, Satana." Eerie black eyes, without orbs and no reflection, flicked to glance past my shoulder. Apparently he saw my companion because the demon's next words weren't so jovial. "I see you've found yourself a human lap dog."

Auric didn't help matters by growling again.

I tsked Azazel, Satan's lieutenant, and my former suitor. Actually, suitor depended on how you looked at it. Azazel wanted me; I had just never wanted him. Something he still had a problem grasping, hence my caution where he was concerned.

"Have you grown so lazy that you can't see my protector is more than a mere human?" What we still had to determine.

The large demon sniffed and sneered. "He might have some magic, but I'll bet he bleeds like a human. And screams like one, too."

"If there's any screaming that's going to happen, it will be because of pleasure. The pleasure I give Muriel, asshole."

When Auric spoke, he insulted like a champ. He also knew how to make my heart go pitter-patter. His strong presence at my back also gave me extra confidence and cockiness. "What do you want, Azazel? Did my father send you?"

"That weakling? Lucifer is on his last legs. A new power is coming, and it will sweep your father from his throne, and a new order will prevail in Hell."

"And you're helping this new power?"

"Aiding. Abetting. Killing for." Azazel spat the words and laughed.

"Traitor," I hissed. Knowing my father's trusted lieutenant had betrayed him boiled my blood. I fought an urge to step through that door and punish him. However, Azazel was a high-level demon, thus a thread of sanity and self-preservation held me back. But being smart didn't mean I wasn't still pissed. "You'll pay for your change in loyalty," I promised. Perhaps it was my glowing eyes or the nasty smile that curled my lip; either way, Azazel took an unconscious step back.

As if realizing he'd shown weakness, Azazel puffed his chest and blew smoke out his nose. "You do not have the power to hurt me, Satana. I, on the other hand, can cause you a world of pain." Behind me, Auric growled, and I put my arm up to prevent him from coming forward.

"I'd like to see you try." No, really I would. Azazel was a renowned fighter. Kicking his ass would totally boost my reputation.

"Not today, devil's spawn." Azazel leered, revealing sharp teeth. "Today I've come to offer a deal to Lucifer's daughter. Leave with me now, as my concubine, and you can live."

"No."

Azazel appeared taken aback. "Don't you want to know what will happen if you refuse?"

"Doesn't matter. My answer is still. No. N dot O. No." Would he make me repeat myself?

"Then you die."

I laughed. Sorry, the whole ultimatum thing...it just didn't work for me.

"Listen, Azz; I told you before, and I'm going to tell you again. Not even if you were the last demon on earth. So you can take your offer and shove it up—"

I never got to finish my sentence because, with a scream of rage, Azazel came rushing toward me, only to hit an invisible wall. The magic around my apartment, which even my powers couldn't undo, stopped him, that and the sword point Auric shoved into his belly. Even Azazel, an old and powerful demon, couldn't handle the slice of blessed metal.

"Enough talk." Auric, with a grim look, pushed me aside and shoved the length of blessed steel deeper into Azazel's flesh as he stepped out into the hall.

"Auric! No, come back in here," I cried, worried he'd get hurt. Being a man, he, of course, ignored me.

"How nice. The squishy human has come out to play." Azazel grinned evilly, the wound in his belly painful, but not incapacitating. With a snap of his fingers and a hissed word, a magical blade of gleaming black fog appeared in his hand.

I knew that sword. A slice from its edge was deadly. And I was rather fond of Auric.

With a shrug, I stepped out into the hall, too, and laughed at Azazel's look of frustration because Azazel's magical blade—specially made by a *human* wizard—wouldn't appear in my presence. Being overly confident, he hadn't thought to bring a real one for backup.

"Get back in the apartment," Auric grunted, trying to pull his sword up the demon's body in an attempt to eviscerate it.

"Not until you do," was my stubborn reply. I dodged to avoid a claw Azz swiped at me.

Auric realized his blade wouldn't move any farther and pulled it out, its shiny length covered in dark blood. He spun its sharp length at the demon, who danced back.

"I am trying to protect you."

"I don't need protection," I huffed, landing a kick

on Azazel's kneecap. *Crack*. The leg buckled, but the demon didn't go down.

"Muriel, if this relationship is going to work, then I'm going to expect you to listen to me."

I snorted. "Good luck with that." If my dad never succeeded, what made him think he could? Wait a second. Had he said the word relationship? My sudden shock saw me almost lose part of my face. Good thing Auric managed to block the swipe.

"Dammit, woman! Get back in the apartment," Auric shouted, swinging his sword and scoring a slice across Azz's corded arm.

"No!" I wasn't about to leave the guy who wanted a relationship with me to fight alone. I dropped to the floor and rolled toward Azz's legs. As soon as I hit the leathery skin, I punched up, hard, into his jewels. Yes, demon balls were just as sensitive as a man's.

With a scream of frustration—and quite a bit of pain—Azazel called up a portal and dove into it. I almost followed him through. I wanted to meet this supposed new master who thought he could steal my dad's demons. More important though, I wondered if Dad knew about Azazel defecting to the other side. Another thing to tell him when I saw him.

My head popped up as I heard the sound of a

door opening farther up the hall. A wrinkled face, framed in curlers, peered out.

I gave my neighbor, ninety-year-old Miranda, a fake smile. "Darn door-to-door telemarketers. They just don't know how to take no for an answer." I doubted she believed me, but she ducked back into her apartment quicker than a bunny into a burrow.

The subterfuge that seemed to be a daily part of my life, not to mention the danger that came with just being me, suddenly fatigued me. Why couldn't I just live a normal life? All I wanted to do was crawl under my covers, go to bed, and forget about everyone and everything.

Well, maybe not Auric. I still wanted him—and, lucky me, he hadn't run away. He slid his sword back in its sheath, and then he picked me up in those deliciously muscled arms and carried me back into the apartment.

"You don't have to carry me. My legs work."

He ignored me as he headed straight into my bedroom with my not-so-impressive bed. He laid me down gently on the covers. Head pillowed, I watched him as he pulled off my boots and socks. The tender caring he displayed seemed so strange, coming from such a warrior. But I liked it.

"You don't have to stay," I repeated again.

Auric just shot me a look and snorted. "If ever there was someone in need of a full-time bodyguard, it's you." He pulled off his own boots and socks and placed them alongside. I found it strangely intimate. Next, his sword sheath came off. He laid it within easy reach, propped against the bed, a bed he still intended to share, apparently.

With a lazy smile and a heated gaze that made my mouth dry and my heart patter faster, he popped the top button on his jeans before he lay down beside me on the bed.

The bed dipped under his weight, and I found myself sliding toward him. I could have stopped myself, but I craved the warmth of his body, even as I came to grips with the oddity of lying in bed with a man.

My body ended its slide tucked against his side, nestled under his arm, which he draped above the top of my head and pillow. This intimate sharing made me tongue-tied and shy, not to mention much too aware of his body.

Me, without a thing to say? And my dad said Hell would freeze over first.

"What's it like being the daughter of the most infamous man in the world?" Auric asked, breaking the silence.

My laughter emerged more high-pitched and brittle than I would have liked. I loved my dad, don't get me wrong, but some days, it wasn't easy being Satan's daughter. "You really want to know?"

Auric turned on his side and faced me. "Tell me."

So I did.

"I came to live with my dad, in Hell, when I was about five. I don't really remember anything before that. It's like my memories were wiped for those years. It wasn't all bad. My dad set aside a wing in his palace for me. I had a human nanny, hellhounds, lots of demonlings my age, and my dad."

"He actually raised you?" Auric sounded surprised.

"Of course he did." But it was a valid question. Most of my siblings lived with their mothers. I didn't have one. I had him. "Daddy always made sure to spend time with me every single day. My dad might be Satan, and he'd deny it, but he loves me." Why that fact seemed to surprise everyone, I didn't know. Even bad guys could love.

"I'm sorry; I guess I just never pictured Lucifer as being the fatherly type."

"Well, I didn't say he did things like normal human fathers did, but he tried his best."

It made me think about my eighteenth birthday. An age when most parents were teary-eyed over their little girl getting older and begging her not to grow up so fast.

My dad asked why I was still a virgin.

I told him none of the boys measured up to him, something I laughed about later when he couldn't see me. But that conversation started the parade of men, in all shapes, sizes, and species, as the king of Hell tried to help me lose what he considered a handicap. My succubi sisters looked at me strangely, too. Sex was just sex, they told me. Who cared if love was involved?

I did.

To make Satan happy, for my twentieth birthday, I got a tattoo above my buttocks. Of course, the fact that I'd gotten a pink butterfly didn't impress him, but he seemed pleased that I'd at least made a step in the direction of depravity and corruption.

Auric interrupted my tale. "Show me."

Lacking inhibitions, I rolled onto my stomach and pulled down my pants, flashing my little butterfly at him.

I trembled when he traced its shape with his finger.

"Nice," he said, his voice thick.

I wondered if he meant the tattoo or my ass. I kind of hoped the latter.

Trying to fight the carnal thoughts that continued to plague me, I decided it was time for him to bare all.

I flipped onto my back and found him staring at me intently, like some kind of puzzle he still hadn't quite figured out. What could I say? I had depth.

"Your turn," I stated.

"I don't have any tattoos."

"Don't play stupid. What's your story? What are you?"

"Just a man with a magic sword."

I didn't like the way he kept evading my questions, a thought I lost track of when he suddenly rolled on top of me. The full-length contact made me flush with heat and sent my tummy flip-flopping.

"What are you doing?" I asked, trying to sound outraged, but instead it came out breathy.

"This." He dipped his head down and tasted me. Unlike the soft kisses of before, this one had strength in it. He took my lips as if he owned them, tasting and caressing them with his own until I moaned in pleasure. My hands twined themselves in his ebony hair as I kissed him back, just as passionately. The soft strands tickled like silk between my fingers. I yanked on two fistfuls, and he let go of my lips.

"What are you doing?" I whispered again as my heart raced erratically.

"Getting to know you better." He grinned mischievously. "I give you my word, though; no matter how wild you get, I won't breach your maidenhead. Trust me."

Trust me. I looked into his vivid green eyes and wondered if I could.

"Trust me," he murmured again as he leaned back down to catch my lower lip between his teeth.

Oh, why the heck not? If this wildness I felt for Auric wasn't love, then what was it?

I wanted to find out.

Let me feel what love is.

I let go of his hair and wrapped my arms around his torso, feeling the muscles in his back rippling as he held most of his weight off me. He braced himself on his forearms, but I wanted to feel his body crushing mine. We were clothed; how dangerous could it be?

I chopped his arms so he collapsed on top of me, and I found out just how dangerous. The feel of his groin, a bulging hardness pressing against the vee of my thighs, had me arching my hips against his. My breathing came even faster, mixed with mewling sounds as his mouth left my swollen lips to travel down to nibble on my neck. I writhed beneath him as he caressed the soft, sensitive skin there. I knew I should tell him to stop, but my mouth refused to speak.

When his lips moved even lower, my hands came up to push him away. Yet again, my body betrayed me as I dug my fingers into his shoulders and arched my back instead of shoving him off. I didn't want the pleasure suffusing me to stop.

His tongue traced the curve of my shirt's neckline while his hand cupped one of my breasts. The pad of his thumb brushed over my nipple, which immediately hardened into a point. That nub tightened even more when he grasped it with his teeth. I cried out at this new experience and dug my fingers even deeper into the muscles of his shoulders. The fabric of my T-shirt became wet as he sucked at my nipple, drawing it out.

I couldn't control my moans. The feel of his mouth, even through the material, sent a hot jolt of desire right down to my pussy. I could feel my panties getting damper and damper while a pressure built inside me, greater than anything I'd ever experienced.

As if sensing my growing urgency, he slid sideways so he only partially covered me, and his hands skimmed my lower stomach. I trembled at his touch and almost bucked him off when his nimble fingers slid under the waistband of my yoga pants.

My conscience felt a twinge of worry at this point. Would he keep his word? But he remained clothed, even as his fingers tangled in my curls down below. Then he distracted me from his hand when his mouth resumed its torture of my breasts. His teeth nipped the bud and wrenched a cry from me.

A cry I repeated when his finger found my swollen nub below. My whole body arched off the bed when he began stroking me, his rough finger creating a delicious friction on this most sensitive of spots. I knew I should push him away, as the feelings he provoked raged out of control. Instead, I said, "Please," a word he swallowed with his lips as he changed position, his possessive mouth branding mine.

I thrashed on the bed in pleasure. I wanted, no, needed, more. The waves of bliss inside me kept building, almost painfully so. I didn't protest when I felt his lips slide from mine, licking their way down my neck. They slid down the length of my chest to my lower belly. For a moment his fingers stopped their torture, but only for a second as he slipped my pants down, pulling them off me so rapidly that I didn't even have a chance to protest.

Then I didn't even think of protesting as he put his hot mouth on my sex. Actually, I screamed. I'd read about oral sex, even fantasized about it, but nothing had prepared me for the total fucking pleasure of it.

His tongue flicked across my clit, an exquisite feeling that he followed up with a full-on suck.

I bucked, my hips coming high off the bed. One strong hand pushed me back down; and as he held me there, a prisoner to his mouth, I felt his other hand stroking my inner lips. I quivered when he slid first one, then two, and finally a third finger partially in. I clenched tightly around those penetrating fingers and heard him grunt as he continued to bathe my clit with his tongue.

I rode the roller coaster of bliss at this point. Out of control, screaming at the thrill, until finally I reached the top of that big hill and crested it. What followed was a pure rush, one that made me scream and shake, as the most powerful orgasm I'd ever experienced ripped through my body.

But Auric didn't stop the torture there; oh no, he held me down and continued flicking my swollen nub with his tongue until my body was so sensitized it convulsed again. The ripples of my second orgasm almost made me black out, and when I came back down from that high, I found myself trembling, and yet also feeling strangely energized.

All of me hummed. Hummed with a languorous power. Was this what they meant when they talked about an afterglow?

No wonder sex was so addictive. Then again, that hadn't been sex, only a prelude. I wondered just how much greater the act would feel. If I weren't such a boneless mess, I might have been tempted to find out.

Auric moved around until he lay beside me again. He turned me onto my side and pulled me into him, spooning me. He said nothing, which I mentally thanked him for because I didn't know what I would have said. "Thank you" seemed kind of inadequate.

I marveled at his self-control, though, because, even through his clothing, I could feel his erection pressing against my backside. The man was hard as a freaking rock.

That made me feel a little guilty; should I have reciprocated? I still couldn't believe he'd kept his word. He'd pleasured me while respecting my vow of no sex.

The only thing that nagged me was the thought I'd broken my vow, even without the penetration. Semantics, perhaps, but it bothered me. Did I love Auric? If he'd tried to fuck me, would I have let him?

The answer scared me.

CHAPTER TWELVE

Despite everything, and the million questions still running through my mind, I managed to fall asleep. And I dreamed. Wet dreamed to be precise.

Should I blame Auric's presence for my erotic dreams, where I did naughty things to him and he did naughty things back?

In the midst of a particularly gymnastic feat, I was abruptly awoken by a shout.

"Muriel! How do you work this damnable coffee machine?"

Crap, my father had arrived. Bad for a few reasons.

One. He had a tendency of wrecking my coffee makers because he just couldn't figure them out. But problem number two might prove worse.

I glanced at my bed, and noted no hot sleeping hunk in it. My initial reaction? Relief. Auric had left, which meant daddy wouldn't catch him. So why was that relief quickly followed by disappointment?

Because I couldn't believe he'd just left like that. Without a note or a kiss goodbye or... A horrifying thought hit me.

What if Auric had stayed and now faced an irate king of Hell?

I scrambled out of bed and took only a second to yank on my pants and tuck down my shirt before I sped out to the living room. I skidded to a stop when I saw my dad stood alone, coffee cup in hand, glaring at my Keurig.

My body relaxed as a lot of anxious tension eased out of me. Saved—for the moment, that is.

"Satana Muriel Baphomet, just what have you been up to?" Satan asked in a quiet, controlled voice.

Oh-oh, that sounded like trouble. So, of course, I played dumb. Never admit to anything. A rule my daddy taught me. "What do you mean, Daddy dearest?"

As I walked around to the couch, I noted Auric's leather duster sitting on it. Damn. I sat down quickly, trying to cover it while mentally panicking. If the coat was here, then Auric hadn't left after all, which meant...

My eyes strayed to the closed bathroom door, and now that I was listening for it, I noted the muted sound of the shower running. I had to get my father out of here quickly before Auric came out, or there would be hell to pay, literally.

"Don't act dumb with me," the lord of the pit said in that still-quiet tone. "I know you had a man here last night. Charon told me." His face then broke out into a delighted smile. "And he's still here, which means you finally did it! Such a good girl. So who's the lucky chap?"

Damn, Dad thought I'd finally gotten deflowered. Talk about an awkward conversation to have, and before coffee, too. "Not so fast, Dad. Yes, a man did stay over last night, but nothing happened. We just talked." And he gave me the wickedest orgasm ever, but some things you just didn't tell your father.

Lucifer's brows shot up. "What do you mean you just talked? Where is this idiot? I'm going to have a talk with him about defiling my daughter. Maybe he needs pointers."

"Dad!" I squealed. "That is so gross. And he doesn't need any help. I told you I'm not having sex until I'm in love. Now, do you mind changing the subject? This is so none of your business." Not to mention mortifying.

"I'm your father. Everything about you is my business."

"Not this," I muttered through clenched teeth. The bathroom door thankfully stayed shut, the sound of the shower still evident, and that kind of surprised me. For a guy determined to protect me, Auric didn't seem too observant. Like, hello, biggest demon of all in my living room.

I needed to get my mind back on track. "Dad, what's this about an uprising going on? And why did I have to hear about it from Charon?"

"Bah, that puny attempt at rebellion?" my dad scoffed. "I squash a dozen of those a week. This one's just taking a little longer than usual. However, I do need you to be a little more careful. Apparently, these applicants to eternal torture seem to think they can hurt me by killing you. Rubbish, of course, but I thought you should know."

I smiled. Dad hated public displays of affection. "Ridiculous. Don't they know you only care about yourself?"

"That's me. Totally selfish. And because I'm selfish and wealthy and able to flaunt it, if you need any guards, I can spare a couple. Not that I care about your well-being or anything," he said in a gruff tone, not deigning to look at me.

I looked at him, though, in his neatly pressed Armani suit. A picture of gentlemanly elegance if one ignored his hair curling into horns and the evil penguins on his tie.

"No need to give me a protection detail. You keep them in Hell where they can keep an eye on the downtrodden. I've got it covered over here. Which reminds me, you do know Azazel has jumped the fence and is helping your opponent, right?"

Lucifer's face darkened. "Traitor! And after all I've done for him. I'll reserve a special punishment for him."

"Very good." My heart practically stopped as sudden panic hit me due to the fact that I no longer heard the shower. "Well, if that was all you had to tell me, then you should get back home. I'm sure you're needed to crush a few spirits, maybe ruin a few dreams, torture a few worthy damned souls."

Satan frowned at me. "Muriel, are you trying to get rid of me?"

"Me?" I opened my eyes wide. "Don't be silly."

The king of Hell looked at me suspiciously, but I kept smiling brightly. Finally, he let out a sigh. "Oh, I almost forgot." He snapped his fingers. "You are so grounded," he boomed, loud enough that the picture frames on the wall shook.

"What?" I squeaked. "Why?"

"I am not just your father; I am the lord and master of deceit. Did you really think I wouldn't find out about you consorting with that–that–"

"Are you talking about me?" asked Auric in a deadly quiet voice from behind me.

I wanted to bang my head against the wall. Damn, and double damn. I could see this getting ugly real quick as the testosterone level inched up into dangerous levels. Not to mention my arousal levels, as Auric's shirt clung damply to the well-defined muscles of his chest.

"Listen, Dad, I know you told me to stay away from him, and well, I, um, failed."

"Evidently. But you really should have tried harder. There was a reason for my warning." My father smiled slyly. "Has he told you just who and what he is?"

A sick feeling formed in my stomach as I glanced from my father's gleeful face to Auric's tight one. I just knew I wouldn't like what was coming.

"I was planning to tell her myself."

Tell me what?

"When? After you took her heart and virginity?"

said Satan, pulling the protective father routine, to my surprise.

I'll be damned. Wait, I was. Auric flushed a beet red. Wait, did that ruddy color mean my father was right? Was Auric planning to debauch me? Mmm, how titillating. But back to the matter at hand.

"What are you hiding?" Arms crossed over my chest, I faced Auric.

"It's not as bad as Satan is making it out to be." No, it must be worse judging by how unhappy he appeared.

"Great, if it's not so bad, then tell me." What was the big fucking secret? Auric was married. *Not for long, I'll make him a widower.* He used to be a girl. I was open to other lifestyles. My mind ran through the many possibilities, but I couldn't see many that would change how I felt.

He'd had opportunity to kill me but hadn't.

He definitely wasn't happy to see my father.

So what? What was the freaking secret?

Auric looked from me to Lucifer. On his face, I could read the inner battle he fought, a battle he lost. Sighing, he said, "I'm an angel."

Okay, not the answer I'd expected.

"A fallen one," interjected my father.

I shot my dad an evil look. "Let him tell me, Dad. I want to hear it from his lips."

"I am an angel, fallen from Heaven and a former soldier in the Army of Light."

"Big deal. What's the problem? We've got lots of fallen angels in Hell." Most of them drunks whining about how they missed the good ol' days.

"Yes, we do get many misbehaving angels," said my father gleefully. He took special pleasure in corrupting his brother's army of light. "But the fallen you've met in Hades are those who arrived because they took a deal. They committed horrible sins. Their souls have been lost beyond redemption. In other words, they belong to me."

I wrinkled my forehead and tried to process what they both weren't telling me. I hated intense early morning discussions, especially before my daily cup of coffee. Slowly, the light bulb lit up inside my head, and understanding dawned. "You haven't lost your soul to the dark side yet, which means you can still redeem yourself in the eyes of God and resume your position in Heaven. Well, that's good for you, isn't it?"

Auric looked miserable.

"Come on, tell her the rest," goaded my father.

"I can return if I perform a great act of good." The words emerged reluctantly.

I could be really dense at times. "Like what, saving an old lady from a burning building?"

"Bigger." Auric shifted uncomfortably.

And then I had the big revelation. My mouth dropped open, and my eyes widened, and I whispered, "If you rid the world of a great evil. Something like, say, Satan's daughter."

"Originally, I'd planned that; but then I met you and got to know you and..."

"You wanted to kill me!" I shrieked.

"Not anymore." Auric looked at me pleadingly.

"Oh, gee, that makes it all better. So, what, you're going to kill one of my friends instead? Maybe my sister Bambi?" I ranted.

"No, of course not. I—" Auric stumbled over his words, his eyes a window into misery, but I didn't care.

I felt so betrayed. I'd trusted him. Allowed myself to start caring for him. Let him touch me. And all along he'd been lying.

"Well, I see my work here is done," said my all-too-cheerful father, rubbing his hands. "I'll talk to you later." With a pop and a stink of brimstone,

Satan called a rift and returned to Hell to spread around some more of his version of joy.

Meanwhile, my heart shriveled inside my chest, and the walls that protected my psyche came slamming down. "I think you should leave." I didn't care if my words were wooden. They sounded as dead as I felt. I headed to my bedroom, where I planned to crawl under the covers and cry.

"Can't we at least talk about this?" he asked, reaching for my arm.

Without even conscious thought, I repelled him. My power lashed out and pushed him back hard enough to hit the wall and crack it. He stared at me, surprised, which made two of us. I mean I knew I had power and all, but I'd never had it react like that. Not without a word, or so powerfully.

"Please leave. There's nothing left to say."

Auric looked as miserable as I felt. How dare he! He'd betrayed me.

He. Hurt. Me.

He was lucky I let him live.

I listened, with my back turned, as Auric grabbed his coat and left.

As soon as the door shut behind him, the first of many tears rolled down my face. I clenched my fists at my sides and let out a scream, a gut-wrenching sound that went on and on before I dropped to my knees and sobbed.

How could he have done this to me? I thought he'd cared for me. I'd begun caring for him. I'd told him things I'd never told anyone. Let him touch me in ways I'd never been touched before. And it had all been a lie. A big, fat, fucking lie.

I don't know how long I cried before soft arms cradled me.

"There, there, little lamb," came the soft tones of Bambi. "You forget all about that nasty man."

"He hurt me," I said in a little lost voice. "Why? I was ready to give him my body. I was ready to give him my love." I'd come so close to handing him my soul.

"He's a man." Spoken in a hard voice. "Men are all pigs. Trust me, I know."

"But I thought Auric was different." I hiccupped through my tears. "I thought he saw me as a person. I let him touch me, and I liked it. How could I like it when all along he was planning to kill me?"

"I don't know, little lamb. Are you sure he wanted to kill you?"

I pondered Bambi's question, and my first impulse was to shout, "Yes, of course he did! I'm

Satan's child." But then I started using my brain for something other than filler for my skull.

Now that I thought about it, Auric had been given plenty of opportunities to kill me, had he wanted to. Hell, I'd fallen asleep beside him. Could I have been any more vulnerable than that?

Bambi sensed the change in my mood. "What did you just think of, little sister?"

"Why didn't he kill me?"

"Maybe he was waiting for the right moment."

"That's just it, Bee; he had plenty of opportunity, not to mention a holy sword, but he didn't. Why didn't he kill me and earn back his wings?"

"I'll deny it if you ever repeat this, but I've been around men a long time. I've learned how to read them. If I had to wager, I'd say he's in love with you." Bambi's face soured at the word 'love', an emotion succubi used to their advantage but didn't understand.

However, that answer, coming from my sister of all people, floored me. Loved me? Could it be possible? And did I love him? I thought I might, but... It would certainly explain the pain that now engulfed me at his betrayal. Actually, it was the answer that made the most sense.

I loved a fallen angel. And I'd thrown him out and told him never to come back.

The tears started rolling again.

"What?" asked Bambi, her brow creased with concern.

"I told the man I love to go away and never come back."

Bambi laughed. "Oh, little lamb, you can't get rid of him that easily."

"What makes you say that?" I sniffled.

"I saw him lurking outside, keeping an eye on the building."

My heart started beating again, only to stutter to an almost immediate halt. "He's probably just waiting for a killer demon to show up so he can do his good deed and go back to Heaven."

Bambi just laughed again and pulled me up from the floor. "Go have a shower while I make some coffee. You'll want to look your best when he comes groveling back."

Somehow I couldn't picture Auric groveling to anyone, but a shower and a caffeine jolt sounded great.

My epiphany came in the shower.

CHAPTER THIRTEEN

I couldn't let Auric love me, not if I loved him. As the daughter of Satan, I would never be welcomed into Heaven, whether I behaved or not. Forget the family discount and forgiveness on sins. Even though God was technically my uncle, he'd never bend the rules.

If I got involved with Auric, by default, he'd find himself banned from Heaven, too. He'd never get his wings back and rejoin his comrades in paradise. He'd never soar high in the sky over a city made of clouds, moonbeams, and sunshine. He'd forever bear the taint of the pit.

If I loved him, I had to let him go.

I didn't cry as long this time; there was something about being noble and self-sacrificing that made one's backbone stronger. I would help save

Auric from himself, and in time, he would hopefully find a way to get back to Heaven that didn't involve killing me. And maybe eventually, I'd find another man who made my knees turn to Jell-O, my heart beat faster, and whom my dad absolutely hated.

After crying a little more, I finally finished showering and then dressed somberly. Pleated, short, black and green plaid skirt; a black blouse unbuttoned far enough to show the black lace of my push-up bra; and sensible, black ballerina flats in case I needed to kick some assassin's ass. I pulled and twisted my hair into a tight chignon, into which I tucked my two long, silver needles. I also put on my thigh sheaths and slid enchanted daggers into them. My bar had a flamethrower under the counter and more weapons in my office if I needed them. And I shouldn't forget my most potent weapon —myself.

When I finally strutted into the kitchen, confidence restored, Bambi smiled and handed me a cup of coffee.

"There's my ferocious lamb," she said with a wide smile. For the world's biggest slut, Bambi was an awesome big sister. And, no, that wasn't an insult; Bambi took pride in winning the title year after year.

"You ready to get your man back?" she asked.

"Nope. I've decided he's better off without me. It's the only way he'll go back to Heaven."

"Are you sure about this?" questioned Bambi, her beautiful face creased in concern.

My voice said, "Yes," but my heart cried, "No." Didn't matter, it had to be done.

As I walked to work beside Bambi, I kept looking for signs of Auric. She assured me he followed us, yet I couldn't sense him.

Good, because that meant I wouldn't have to tell him to find someone else, but disappointing because I had this marvelous speech I'd prepared. The jerk stayed far enough away that I didn't get a chance to use it.

His buddies, David and Christopher, walked into the bar not long after I opened it. My glare must have been in fine form because they looked at their feet, shuffling them sheepishly, not daring to look me in the face.

I snorted. "Let me guess, you were in on it."

"We didn't know it was you," said David. "We thought Satan's daughter would be some mean old hag."

"So, what, you're not going to kill me because I'm young and pretty?"

"Well, yeah." David shot me a smile. "That, and

we can't kill Auric's girlfriend. It wouldn't be right."

I froze for a second. Girlfriend? What had Auric told them?

"When did Auric say I was his girlfriend?" A query asked quietly. My heart thumped as it waited for the answer. Not that I cared because I still had to dump him.

"Just now, outside, when he said to come in and guard you."

Christopher sighed. "David, my friend, you talk too much. Listen. It's true that initially we came to this bar because we'd heard Satan's daughter could be found here, but as soon as Auric realized that you were her, the plan to kill you for his wings got cancelled. Auric cares for you. It's why we're here. He's asked us to be his eyes and ears inside."

"And just where is he?"

"Around," Christopher replied vaguely.

"Great. Good to know. Listen, while you guys stay here and guard the bar, I've got to go out back to do some paperwork."

A lie—wouldn't Dad be proud?—but I didn't want them following me when I went outside looking for Auric. I sneaked out the side door into the alley, where I stood for a moment. Where was Auric skulking, anyway?

I scoffed in the face of subtlety. "Auric," I hollered. I waited impatiently then called his name again. "Aur–"

A hand clamped down over my mouth, so I naturally sank my teeth into it.

"Ow." I knew that gravelly voice. "What did you do that for?"

"Next time, if you don't want to get hurt, identify yourself before grabbing me." Not in the least bit sorry.

"I was trying to keep you quiet so you didn't announce to the whole world you were out here by yourself."

"But I'm not by myself. You're here. Which is why I'm here, to talk to you about being here when you shouldn't be."

I loved the confused look he got on his face. But I couldn't love it. Hence why I was out here.

"Listen, Muriel, if you're trying to tell me to leave, then you can forget it."

I wanted to ask why he wanted to stay, but of course that was when the demons from Hell showed up. They jumped down from the roof of the bar, three hulking brutes that spread out around us.

With the mood I was in, they should have sent more.

I heard the snick of Auric's blade coming out of the sheath, and knowing the demon behind me would be taken care of, or at least kept busy, I smiled at the two facing me.

"Hello, boys, come to play?" I taunted.

The muscle-bound beasts didn't reply; instead, one moved sideways, trying to flank me, while the other advanced on me. My head remained blank of spells and my power dormant. I'd have to actually fight, which suited me just fine. I had a lot of pent-up frustration right now that needed venting.

I didn't wait for the first demon to reach me. I charged him, my silver blades suddenly in my hands, slashing as I ducked under his swinging fists.

Hit! I scored two symmetrical slashes on his ribs before I twirled out again and danced back.

A feral smile split my lips. Words appeared in my mind as my adrenaline spiked. I did a quick chant, and suddenly my two daggers glowed a deep red. I'd imbued them with hell fire, which meant the next time I cut, the wounds would burn and burn and... Well, let's just say it took some powerful magic to stop the burning.

Sensing motion behind me, I ducked just as a meaty, clawed fist swung where my head would have been. Pivoting on one foot, I kicked out with the other into the creature's kneecap, the force of my blow hitting with a loud crack. The demon fell with a cry as his leg collapsed under him.

My jaw dropped for a second. Either I'd gotten stronger overnight or something weird was going on.

I rolled, instinct suddenly controlling my body, and slashed at the downed demon as he tried to grab me. With a howl, he clutched his burning hand to his chest, and I sprang up. I turned to face the other enemy, only to find Auric battling him. I whirled, looking for more danger, and saw Auric's initial opponent in two pieces. A decapitation. Nice.

I swung back to watch the fight, my heart almost stopping when the ugly black demon raked his claws forward across Auric's chest, tearing the cloth and skin, red blood immediately welling.

I found myself engulfed in fury—how dare he harm Auric?—and, without thinking, shouted the powerful words that suddenly appeared in my mind. The force of them rang in the air, and I saw the demon's eyes widen in horror—something I'd never thought to see on one of their faces—before he disintegrated in a shower of black ash.

But whatever I'd done had been too much, and I collapsed to the dirty asphalt in a faint. The shame of it.

CHAPTER FOURTEEN

When I came to, Auric's face hovered over mine, a concerned look on it.

"Where am I?" I asked, trying to sit up.

Auric put a hand on me and pushed me back down. "On the couch in your office. Stay down for a minute."

"Why? I'm fine. What happened to the demons?"

"What demons?" asked Auric. "Whatever spell you cast turned all three of them to dust."

I stared at him blankly. I'd done what? "Impossible. I can see, maybe, destroying one with the ancient magic like I did before, but three of that size? No way. No one can do that."

"You did it."

I wanted to call him a liar, but I knew he told the truth. It would also explain why I'd fainted. The amount of magic involved... Well, let's just say it had to be staggering.

But where had all that magic come from in the first place? Had I reached some new magical plateau? Whatever had happened had left me weaker than a kitten, something I discovered when I tried to get up.

My head spun in multiple directions, and my legs buckled, sitting me back hard onto the couch.

Auric hovered over me, concerned. He placed the back of his hand on my forehead, as if checking for a temperature. I didn't have one yet, but if he touched me a little lower... How I could think dirty thoughts when my stomach churned with nausea I didn't know, but suddenly I felt a little better.

"Let me up," I complained.

"No, I'm not watching you fall flat on your face. Whatever you did, it took a lot out of you."

I didn't like being treated like an invalid. Annoyed, I pushed at him. I might as well have been pushing a humongous rock. He didn't move, so I leaned back, sulking.

Auric gave me a long look that I returned. He

sighed and shook his head before sticking his head
out the door and murmuring to someone. A second
later, Christopher and Bambi came in.

"Why are they here?" I asked.

"Something happened outside with that magic
you did. I could tell you weren't quite controlling it.
Look at what happened: instead of just destroying
one demon, you took out three. And yesterday at
your apartment with that other demon... I'm not
blind. I saw the look on your face when you disintegrated it. Something is changing with your magic,
and we need to find out why before you hurt yourself." And others. He didn't need to say it for me to
know he was thinking it.

But there was nothing wrong me, or my magic. It
was maybe evolving, but that didn't mean I was a
menace to society and not in control.

Auric saw the argument coming and dropped to
his knees beside the couch I lay on. He kissed me
soundly, effectively swallowing any protest or denials
I would have made. He didn't stop until Christopher
cleared his throat and Bambi giggled. As for me,
dazed from his embrace, I would have done anything
he asked.

As he smiled at me, a smoky gaze full of erotic

promise, his thumb stroked my now-swollen lower lip. "Chris and Bambi are going to ask you a couple of questions to see if they can figure out what's happening with your magic. Be a good girl and answer them."

"But I'd rather be bad."

"Later. And only if you behave and obey."

His smart-ass—totally male—remark annoyed me. "Obey?" Ha. Not likely.

He sighed. "Don't be so difficult, baby. We need to figure out what's happening with your magic."

"My magic's gotten stronger, so what?"

"Just humor me, please."

Humor him or kill him? I glared at Auric, willing him to go away and leave me alone before something bad happened to him. I also wanted to wrap my arms around him and have him kiss me silly again. There was, in that mix of emotions, also an urge to obliterate those demons again for hurting him.

A part of me also wanted to sob because Auric dared to make me love him when I couldn't have him.

I almost told him to go to Hell. Only one problem. If he went to Hell, I'd probably run into him.

My turn to sigh while three sets of eyes observed

me. It looked as if I wasn't escaping here until I cooperated. "What do you want to know?"

"When did you first get your power?" asked Christopher.

"I've always had it." I still remembered the first time I'd used it. It happened not long after I moved into my dad's palace in Hell. In an effort to socialize me, they'd brought a demon child in for me to play with. That hadn't worked out so well.

The bratty imp stole my favorite dolly and taunted me. I remembered crying and pleading for her to give it back. She didn't. And then she laughed at me.

I recalled the burning rage and the overwhelming desire to make her stop. I growled a word. A word to this day I didn't remember, but I clearly recalled what happened next. The demon girl was grabbed by an almost invisible hand and flung through the air, an impromptu flight that ended when she smacked into a wall.

She stopped laughing. I got my dolly back. And everyone was a lot more careful with me after the incident.

"Has it gotten stronger over the years or stayed steady?"

"I peaked a bit in my teens, but pretty steady since then, until a few days ago."

"Anything changed for you? Diet? Sleep?"

I almost giggled as I thought of the one thing I was suddenly getting.

"What did you just think of?" asked Christopher, his suave persona buried under a much more serious mien.

"I'd rather not say." But I didn't have to since I couldn't fight a blush. My red cheeks gave me away. Bambi shot me a knowing look, touched Christopher on the arm, and gestured to Auric. The three of them went into a huddle.

I could have listened in, but my fuzzy head wasn't in the mood to really concentrate that hard.

It didn't stop me from asking a grumpy, "What's going on?"

No reply. They ignored me and whispered frantically.

"Hello?" I griped. "Over here. Mind telling me what you're all yammering about?"

The three of them separated guiltily, and I glared at them.

Bambi and Christopher stared at Auric, but he leaned against the wall of my office, a smirk on his face. "Don't look at me. I'm not explaining the theory."

"What theory? Can someone tell me what's going on? If I wasn't weak as a newborn hellcat, I'd slap you all around for being so mysterious."

"Well, there's a reason for your current incapacity." Christopher cleared his throat. "Um, well, it seems you've drained your reserve of magic. It's why you feel so weak."

Cue my giant eye roll. "Duh. I think I already figured that one out, Sherlock. Not a big deal. I'll rest up and get it back."

"Yes, well, there's more to recuperating than just taking a nap." Christopher shifted uncomfortably. "Do you know how you build up your magical reserves?"

I smelled something not right here. Why were they all looking at me like I was a bomb about to go off? "I've never thought about it before. The magic's always been there, just stronger since I hit puberty."

"Um, well... Let me see how I should phrase this." Christopher flushed and stared at the wall above my head while Auric's face turned to stone. No help from that quarter.

"Oh, by the hag's hairy tit," interjected Bambi with a flick of her luscious long hair. "What this idiot is having a hard time saying is your magic is sexually based."

"That's impossible, I've always had magic."

"A magic that's grown in power as you begin to explore your sexual nature," Bambi interjected.

"That's crazy. I'm not a succubus. I don't eat souls." At least, I didn't recall munching on any.

"You don't need souls to power your magic."

Then what was I using to fill up my esoteric batteries?

Bambi spelled it out. "Your magic comes from sexual pleasure. You need to be sexually stimulated to build your magic back up and to strengthen it."

I laughed. A laughter which died quickly when I saw Auric's smug face, Christopher's uncomfortable one, and Bambi's amused smile.

"No, that can't be right because I'm a virgin..." I trailed off. A virgin who masturbated a lot and who, the night before, had her most intense sexual experience ever—and suddenly managed to destroy three demons at once.

Hot damn. I was some kind of mutant succubus sorceress. In other words, my father's daughter.

As I absorbed the news, and slapped myself mentally for not having figured it out on my own, my sister placed a hand on my arm. "It's not that bad, little lamb. At least you won't accidentally kill anyone in order to feed your magic." I didn't need Bambi's sad smile to know there were some deaths on her conscience that bothered. "And now that you know, you can recharge those batteries anytime. Like now. Chris and I are gonna go so you can have some alone time." I didn't need her wink to know she expected me to go sexually wild as soon as the door closed.

But did I want to? Before I'd answered that question, Bambi snagged Christopher's arm and dragged him out of my office.

"Well, that was interesting," Auric drawled.

I glared at him. "This is your fault."

"Hey, don't get mad at me." He held up his hands. "It's not my fault you've got nympho magic." Then he laughed.

I tried to stay mad. I really did but...really, nympho magic? I giggled along with him.

When we both finally calmed down, I caught him staring at me with the most serious expression. "I'm sorry I didn't tell you what I was."

Shoot. In all the commotion, I'd forgotten I was mad at him. "You should be sorry." Just because I'd grown up in a world where lies were common didn't mean I appreciated his whopper.

"How can I make this up to you?" His green eyes gazed intently into mine, and I had to look away. I needed to be strong for the both of us.

"You can't make this up to me because it's impossible. We can't be together. I mean, seriously, an angel looking to get his wings and a nymphomaniac princess of Hell?" A wan smile tugged my lips. "It would never work. You need to leave, Auric."

"No."

Stubborn man. "I don't want to be with you." I made an attempt to sound hard and uncaring.

My subterfuge failed.

"Liar." Auric went to his knees in front of me and tilted my chin until I looked at him. "I won't hurt you, Muriel, or lie to you again. I promise."

Why did he have to make this so hard? "You still have a chance to earn back your wings and return to Heaven. If you stay with me, you'll lose that chance. I can't let you do that."

"It's not up to you. You want me. Just like I want you."

But want wasn't a reason to ruin his life...to taint his soul. "Why are you doing this?" I cried. "It's not like you love me. How could you? You're an angel. I'm Lucifer's daughter."

"What if I said I love you and have from the first moment I saw you?"

My heart stuttered. Especially since I didn't sense a lie. But the truth? Impossible. "I don't believe you. I remember our encounters." His arrogance and belligerent attitude. "You sure didn't act like a man in love."

"What, would you have had me go down on bended knee and give you flowery speeches like Christopher or give you big kitten eyes like David? That's not me. It will never be me. Fuck, even this conversation isn't me. I'm not a man who talks about feelings." Auric grimaced, and I wanted to smile. "Meeting you changed everything. My goals. My perceptions..." He stroked my chin with his thumb. "I wasn't looking for love. Then, suddenly, I met you, and it's like I got hit by a truckload of feelings, all of them centered around you. Intrigue. Affection. Protection. I love you, baby."

My heart stopped. I wanted to cry out that I loved him, too, but my love would destroy him. I shook my head in denial. "You said yesterday you liked me. And now you want me to believe it's love."

"I lied. I didn't want to scare you off. You'd just told me you wouldn't lie with a man until you found true love. How would it have looked if I'd said it then? What would you have thought?"

"I would have thought you were trying to get in my pants," I grudgingly admitted.

"Exactly."

"This changes nothing. We still can't be together. You're an angel of light. I'm the daughter of Satan. Talk about oil and water. I won't corrupt your chance to return to Heaven."

"Who says you get to decide?"

Um, like hello, did Auric not get that the world revolved around me? "I get to decide. You can't love me. I won't let you."

"What do I have to do to prove to you I love you and want to be with you?"

"You can't."

"I will." He then took my lips, took them in a fierce storm of passion that I greedily inhaled. This would be the last time I touched him like this. The last time I felt the molten pleasure only he could give me.

A last time that I wished could last forever. But couldn't.

I pushed out of the warm circle of his arms and stood. Feeling stronger—Auric packed a potent kiss— I walked to the door and left my office. As I headed for the bar, I could feel him, a scorching presence, at my back.

I pretended not to see him and busied myself behind the bar with unsteady hands. But Auric refused to be ignored. I saw him walk out into the bar area and whisper something to Trixie, who headed off toward the jukebox.

The music blasting from the speakers stopped, as did the dancers who milled about on the dance floor in confusion. Auric walked swiftly to the center of the dance floor, which cleared at his approach. He raised his hands to get everyone's attention, including mine.

"Anyone who knows me will tell you I hate to sing. But my lady over here," Auric said, nodding in my direction, "loves karaoke. So bear with me as I serenade her, will you? And Muriel"—he zeroed in on me, his green eyes intense—"I'm not leaving, and you can't stop me from loving you."

Then he sang to me, his low, gravelly voice playing across my senses like a finely tuned violin. I didn't quite grasp what he sang with the first few bars, but when he hit the lyrics, I smiled. Fuck me, I even felt tears rolling down my cheeks. Stupid angel —how I loved him.

He stared at me while he serenaded me with an

eighties love song, 'What Does It Take' by Honeymoon Suite. A song so apt I had to wonder if he'd planned this. And when he finished, to rousing applause, I found myself moving toward him.

I had no control. I'd tried to warn him. I'd tried to save him, but I was my father's daughter. Selfishness ran in my genes, and I couldn't fight the pull Auric had on my heart and soul.

So be it. We'd be damned together.

CHAPTER FIFTEEN

I'M NOT SURE HOW WE MADE IT TO MY apartment because, once we locked lips in the bar, everything else blurred. And burned...

We stumbled up the stairs to my place—a safer location, considering the bounty on my head. Shutting the door behind me, Auric pushed me up against it and devoured my lips. My lust, held at bay so long, surged through my body like a ravening beast. I wanted to taste every inch of his body.

I pushed his coat off his shoulders, and it fell in a heap, which he kicked to the side. Scooping me up easily, he strode to my bedroom, tossing me on the bed, his green eyes alight with passion as they watched me. He pulled the hem of his T-shirt up and stripped it off, baring his chest. There were three faint red lines marring his perfection, all that remained of his earlier injury. An injury I'd foolishly forgotten.

With a cry, I went to my knees and leaned forward to touch the red welts, the skin lightly ridged as new scar tissue formed. Scars he'd gotten because of me. Callused hands gripped mine, and I looked up at him, my eyes brimming with tears.

"How could I forget?" I whispered, horrified. "You could have been killed. It's dangerous to be around me. I can't let you do this." I tried to twist around him, to flee the love he so innocently offered me. A love I would surely corrupt, given my pedigree.

But I couldn't escape. Auric wouldn't let me. Instead, he wrapped his arms tightly around me and sat on the bed. He pulled me onto his lap and hugged me close.

"I got injured. Big deal. It happens a lot to me."

"But this one is my fault," I said against his chest.

His fingers grasped my face, and he forced me to look at him. "Muriel, my body is covered in scars. So what? I healed."

"This time. What about the next time? What if they kill you? I couldn't stand that." Now that I knew I loved him, the thought of his death terrified me.

"And what if they kill you?" he replied. "Do you

think I'd fare any better? I've been walking this earth for close to thirty years now since being thrown out of Heaven, not truly caring if I lived or died in my quest to return to a realm that spurned me. Then I met you, and suddenly Heaven pales in comparison. I see things in color again, more vividly than before. I feel alive once more, more alive than I've ever felt, even when I was a part of the Army of Light. Knowing this, would you still push me away?"

I didn't know what to say. The thought of my mere existence being so important to someone else frightened me and, at the same time, elated me. In his eyes, I mattered.

Softly, he stroked my lower lip with his thumb. "I meant what I said. I love you. I would give anything to be with you. It matters not that we've known each other only a few days. It matters not who your father is. All that matters is that I be by your side. That you love me in return. Do you love me?"

Openly crying, I tried to shake my head; I tried to lie. And couldn't. Oh, the irony. Lucifer's daughter, unable to lie, even to save the man she loved. "I love you, too. But—"

He kissed me, hard. "No buts. I'm an old-fashioned male, which means, from now on, I get to call the shots."

I would have protested, but he Frenched me when I opened my mouth. Tired of fighting what we both wanted, I relaxed in his arms. At my unspoken signal, he lay me down on the bed. With deft hands, he stripped me. I felt no shame as he looked upon my body. I knew my curves were lush and beautiful, a fact I saw confirmed in the smokiness of his gaze.

He unbuttoned his jeans and pushed them down, along with his briefs. My eyes widened, and I let out a sound at the sight of his erect shaft. Now there was a tool made for sinning.

Surrounded by ebony curls, it stood proud and thick. I reached for him, and Auric eagerly came to me, his heavy body covering mine, skin to skin.

I let my legs fall apart so his body could nestle between my thighs, and I arched up eagerly against him.

"Patience," he whispered as he drank from my lips. "I want to make your first time a special memory."

I let him take control, contenting myself with touching the parts I could reach—his silky hair, his muscled shoulders. He kissed every inch of my body, starting at my lips and working his way down. The bristles on his jaw chafed deliciously against the delicate skin of my neck. His lips, when they covered my nipple, felt like lava, and the tug of desire that shot from my nipple to my crotch made me cry out. His hand kneaded one breast while his mouth toyed with the other. His lips pulled and sucked at my aureole, making it tight and hard. Then he switched to my other breast and started the torture all over again.

I had to close my eyes. I couldn't watch him without wanting to scream for him to take me. I knew Auric would make me his only when he felt ready.

Finally, his wet mouth traced its way down my belly, inching toward the wet core between my legs. I tensed in anticipation, so he teased me, his lips bypassing my pussy and clit to kiss my soft inner thigh. I pulled my knees up and spread my legs wider, exposing myself, taunting him to taste me. He chuckled between my thighs, and his warm breath tickled me.

"Soon, my sweet Muriel," he murmured. Still nibbling the soft flesh of my thighs, he surprised me when he inserted one finger into my wet cleft. He ran that finger around the edge, almost as if he stretched me.

I cried out when his mouth finally found my clit. He laved it with his tongue and lips, and I could feel my pussy going into mini convulsions, especially when he inserted more fingers into the opening of my sex and stretched me even wider.

With my head thrashing from side to side, I moaned at the exquisite feelings he wrung from my body. And when I finally felt his pulsing thickness nudging my lips, I almost sobbed in relief.

But the feel of him poking me made me think of something—safety. "Um, shouldn't you be putting on a condom or something right about now?" My sex-crazed sisters had drilled the concept of safe sex into me at an early age.

"Angels, even fallen ones, are like vamps and shape shifters. The diseases of mortal men have no hold on us."

And I was on the pill, which meant not even a thin layer of latex would dare to dull the feel of him inside me. "In that case then, what are you waiting for?"

Our little conversation, though, had slowed things down, something he quickly remedied when he latched his mouth onto my nipple and sucked, while the tip of his prick rubbed against me. In no time at all, he had me mindless again, and panting.

"Please." I wasn't ashamed to beg. I wanted him so badly it almost hurt.

He braced his body above me and paused. I

opened my eyes slowly and looked at him through heavy lids.

"I love you, Muriel." A declaration he made with his green eyes shining, the truth in his words and expression shaking me to the core.

Then he thrust into me, and I cried out.

The pain I experienced when he breached my maidenhead was, thankfully, brief and minor—it had been more the suddenness that had made me cry out. He stopped moving after pushing himself past my torn barrier, and now that the shock had worn off, I could feel him inside me, impossibly big, but oh, so right.

I pulled him down to me for a kiss, and he groaned against my mouth as he kissed me back, hotly. He began to pump me with his slick length. Short jabs in and out, which felt so good. I writhed, moving my hips to match his rhythm. Close to the brink, I almost cried when he pulled out completely. He teasingly rubbed the head of his cock against my wet slit then drove himself back in, making me scream. It felt so fucking good.

Now he stroked me long and hard, his thick shaft penetrating and retreating, filling me up and making me shudder. Each time the tip of his cock hit the bottom of my womb, I could feel a jolt of pleasure. I wrapped my legs around him, locking him within my body. He pumped me harder and faster until, like a high note held too long, I shattered, screaming his name.

My nails clawed at his back as wave after orgasmic wave crashed through my body. His body went taut seconds later, and Auric let loose a long groan and a final thrust. I felt a spurting heat deep within me, signaling he'd found his pleasure, too.

As I listened to the distant sound of fireworks—a coincidence?—I folded myself tightly around him, my face buried in his shoulder, tears leaking from the corners of my eyes. I felt so blissfully happy at this moment and so in love that it hurt.

Tender lips kissed my temple, my nose, my cheeks.

The caresses stopped.

"Why are you crying?" He sounded utterly horrified. He quickly rolled off me, and I opened my eyes. "Are you all right? Did I hurt you?" Anguish colored his expression.

I smiled at him a little blearily. "I'm not hurt. Just so happy right now."

"Oh." At my admission, he settled down beside me and pulled me into him for a body-to-body hug.

"Is it always that good?" I asked, letting my fingers dance over this chest.

"It's never been that good."

"Really?" I propped up on one elbow to look at him. "You mean I'm the best you've ever had?"

"The best and, from now on, the only one I will ever have."

I pinked, something I did often around my angel. "When can we try it again?"

Auric cocked a brow at me and smiled, a slow, sexy, sinful look that made me wet and horny all over again.

"I'm ready when you are," he said. "But, first, let's get you washed up."

I looked down and saw the blood that signaled I had finally, fully, become a woman.

Bye-bye, virginity.

Grinning at the view of the tight buttocks that walked into my bathroom, I sure was glad I'd waited for the right man.

Since I wasn't going back to sleep, I hopped off the bed. My body thrummed with energy. I wondered, with quite a bit of interest, if my shower was big enough to play in. Auric took up a lot of space, a fact I liked, but in the tight confines of my shower, that could make things tricky. But I was still willing to try.

The water was running, and he stood under the spray when I walked in. He held the curtain aside and moved back so I could stand under the water. Thick arms wrapped around me from behind, and his hands cupped my breasts, lifting and squeezing them. I wiggled my bottom at him and felt a hot poker answer me back. I leaned my head back into his shoulder; he dipped forward and sucked on my neck. My knees buckled, making me glad he had his arms around me to support me. But I hadn't only planned on him playing with me. I'd waited a long time for *the one*. Having found him, I had to touch him and desperately needed to taste him.

I turned in his arms, letting our tongues tangle for a moment, before pulling back and pressing my lips to the hollow at the base of his neck. I slid my hands up his sides to his pecs then placed them there, palms flat, fingers spread, feeling his heat and even his heartbeat against them. His nipples were already puckered, and they tempted me to nibble. I leaned forward and bit one lightly. Auric tightened his hands around my waist, and I smiled. I licked him like he'd licked me. But something kept poking me, something hard and delicious.

I needed to explore. I let my lips slide down his torso. I heard Auric suck in a hard breath when I came even with his cock. I reached out a hand and stroked it lightly. It jerked in response. I looked up and saw Auric staring down at me, his eyes glazed with desire.

My lips curved into a wicked smile, and I licked them. I touched him again, wrapping my hands tightly around him this time. He sighed and tilted his head back. Pleased at his response, I stroked his silky cock, back and forth. The thickness and length of it fascinated me. The head, swollen and blushing with color, tempted me. I stuck out my tongue and flicked it against his knob. Auric made a strangled cry, and his hands tangled in my hair.

Emboldened, I slid my lips over the soft skin of his cockhead, taking him into my mouth. The fingers in my hair tightened, and this excited me. I slid him deeper into the warm recesses of my mouth. My hand grasped the base of his cock tightly so that all of him would be covered because it just wouldn't all fit in my mouth. The rest of his cock I fucked with my mouth. In and out. The slick length of his penis grazed my teeth, and somehow he seemed to get bigger, making my mouth feel smaller. He gripped me tightly, helping me bob my head. I moaned, a sound that came out gargled because of the prick I sucked.

I discovered that giving him pleasure went two ways. It also made me wet and wild. With my free hand, I stroked myself, my fingers slippery with my juices and the water that still poured on me from the shower.

Auric's body went stiff, and I wondered if he'd shoot into my mouth—I wanted to taste him. But instead of feeding me his essence, he pulled his cock away from my lips and said hoarsely, "Enough."

He pulled me up from my kneeling position and, cupping my ass cheeks, lifted me and leaned me against the shower wall before impaling me with his thick, hard shaft. I wrapped my legs around his waist, this new position thrilling me, as it showcased how powerful Auric truly was. He held me effortlessly and pumped me, his throbbing cock driving hard and deep.

I mewled in his arms, my pussy clenching tightly around him. Exquisite pleasure built inside me. I squeezed him with my pelvic muscles and panted harshly as he penetrated me over and over. With a bellow, he came, his hard cock pulsing and squirting hotly inside me, a sensation that sent me over the edge. I screamed as I orgasmed in his arms. Together we collapsed in the bottom of the tub, me draped bonelessly over his lap. Even in our pleasure-weakened state, he still held me protectively, cradling me like the most precious of objects.

I reveled in the feeling that, in a way, made me feel closer to him than the actual sex. Cradling my naked, wet body, Auric stood up, his hard thigh muscles tensing. He rinsed me under the warm water, unwilling to let me go. He stepped out of the tub and wrapped the big fluffy towels that I indulged in around us before he carried me back to the bedroom.

We lay spooned in my bed, skin-to-skin, sated for the moment, but I felt far from tired. My body hummed with power while my mind spun with curiosity.

"Tell me about Heaven?" I asked. I was curious about this paradise everyone aspired to and that he'd given up for me. Could it truly be as wonderful as everyone thought? I would never know. My uncle had never invited me for a visit.

"What is Heaven like?" he mused aloud. "I guess one way to describe it would be like a sunny day that never ends."

"Sounds pleasant," I remarked.

"For a while. I discovered that, without the rain

and the cold and the myriad other things that are the usual part of life, it was hard to appreciate the same perfection, day after day. It's like eating the exact same meal three times a day for the rest of your life. You get tired of it."

"It sounds dull."

"It is. But that's the way it is and always has been. Heaven doesn't like change," he said, bitterness lacing his words.

I sensed a story here. "Why did you get kicked out of Heaven and the Legion of Light?" What I really wondered was, had he done something naughty?

Auric sighed. "It was stupid, really. I got tired of Heaven, of the stagnancy of life there. Of their placidness when it came to the misery and suffering of the world. I demanded to know why we sat by idly while evil, in the form of petty wars, drugs, and abuse, prevailed on earth."

"And their answer?"

"Not our problem. It was mankind's duty to find the right path and suffer if need be. Never mind that a child caught in a crossfire not of their making was maimed or killed. I was told to sit back, relax, and enjoy Heaven and its endless sunshine."

"But surely the Legion of Light does more than that? I've heard my father complain about them."

"Oh, we've had minor skirmishes with your father's demons and henchmen. But again, even there, the rules of engagement are strict. Demons are free to roam the earth causing mischief, and we only get involved if they attack one of our own or encroach upon the Kingdom of Heaven."

"But that's dumb," I exclaimed as I sat up. "I mean I'm not all that keen on the idea of the Army of Light chasing down my dad and his legion, but shouldn't Heaven's army be a little more proactive?"

"You would think. And that's what I said, over and over again. I finally got tired of being ignored, so I tried to do something about it. I came to earth and tried to make a difference. I could only do so much. After all, one angel that can't reveal its identity is no match for the evil that is perpetrated daily. But I tried, and I was called back to stand trial for my actions."

I listened in disbelief. This was Heaven? All my life, I'd expected something more. Something grander. But it sounded like the politics and machinations of Heaven were no better than my father's. At least my father was honest about it, though. Funny, the Devil being honest.

Seriously, though, my father took an active part in the world. Yes, his minions tended to lead people down the path of misdeeds, but perhaps if the angels of Heaven did more to encourage people to follow the path of light, Hell wouldn't be so crowded.

And contrary to belief, living in the pit wasn't that bad. Sure, some people got eternally tortured, but we were talking the worst of the worst here, the Hitlers and Attilas of the world. Most regular folk who died and went to Hell still lived a regular life. They still loved and lived and struggled. They just didn't have to worry anymore about following some stupid code.

I looked at Auric, and I knew how his story in paradise ended. "They found you guilty."

"Unanimously so. They took my wings and almost all my powers and cast me down to earth. However, they decided that, as I hadn't yet trod the path of evil, I should be given a chance to redeem myself. If I performed an act of great good, rid the world of a huge evil, I'd be welcomed back into Heaven."

"So you came up with the plan to kill the Devil's daughter."

"Not at first. At first, I was pissed and relieved. I now had the freedom to help whomever I wanted, and I did. But again, no matter how much I tried, people still chose the easier path."

"Maybe because Heaven's path is too complicated," I said out loud. Oops. I wanted to slap my hand over my mouth, but Auric smiled ruefully.

"You're right. It is too complicated."

"If their policies sucked and you were so bored, then why did you want to go back?"

"I didn't, really. It just occurred to me that, maybe if I did rid the world of an evil figure, perhaps the world would be a little better."

"Because I am so evil." I couldn't help but snort.

Auric's arms wrapped around me tightly, and he laughed. "Yes, you're evil, but in a way I never expected. A good way. I met you, a real princess of Hell, and suddenly the perceptions I'd been taught in Heaven didn't hold true, and I found myself guilty of the same prejudices I had fought against. I judged you without proof. As soon as I met you and talked to you, I realized you were no more evil than I was. You're just a regular person, trying to live life to the best of her abilities."

I took offense at regular—I thought I was pretty super myself. "I am not ordinary!"

"No, you're not; I think you're pretty extraordinary, but the point I was making was that you weren't some malicious, cackling hag spreading evil through the world. And, on that same note, your father isn't as evil as I took him to be."

"Oh, my dad is plenty evil," I corrected.

"But he cares," said Auric. "It never occurred to me the Devil could love, and yet he loves you, his daughter."

"Don't let my dad hear you say that; he doesn't like to admit to those kinds of things."

Auric laughed. "I'll bet he doesn't. It would ruin his reputation and make more of us question Heaven's true purpose and doctrine."

"Does anyone ever make it to Heaven?" From what he'd told me, it seemed almost impossible.

"Some do, but the numbers are small, which is why I never understood the standoff approach."

"Let me ask you one last question." This frank discussion had opened my eyes wider than I would have thought possible. "Do you still want to go back to Heaven?"

"Honestly?" He squeezed me tight while my heart paused its beating to hear his answer. He didn't even hesitate. "No. I don't want to go back. I'm not saying I want to walk a path of evil and join your father's hordes, but neither do I want to return to Heaven and the boredom of my life there. If I could be anywhere, I would stay on this mortal plane with you by my side, trying to make a difference when I can."

"Are you sure that's what you want, though, Auric? We've only spent one night together. There might still be a chance for you to walk away and go back. If you stay with me, you will lose that chance forever."

"I've found a Heaven I love more, here with you," he whispered then turned my face to kiss me.

I kissed him back. He'd assuaged my guilt about loving him, and I forgot about my plan to push him away. Hurting him would be wrong. He'd been betrayed enough, and with my love, I wanted to right those wrongs. Perhaps together we could make a difference.

I lost my train of thought as his lips parted mine and his tongue delved into the recesses of my mouth. Energized by our talk, I kissed him back fiercely. I'd given myself to him before, but to me, it'd had a bittersweet edge, as I'd expected to have to push him away. Now that I knew he was here to stay, that he would be mine forever, I gave it my all. I opened my heart and let him fully in.

We wrestled for dominance on the bed. I tried to push him on his back to explore him again.

"My turn this time," he said with promise; and using his superior male strength—which I loved—he held my hands above my head, making my breasts stick out proudly, the nipples already pointy nubs waiting for his mouth.

Auric liked to tease, I'd noticed, and he did so again, hovering his mouth over my breast, blowing warmly on it then grazing his rough stubble on the soft skin. My breathing sped up, and I twisted in his grip, arching my back, thrusting myself at him. He just chuckled and continued to feather my skin until my whole body, just like a live wire, thrummed with passion and energy.

Turning sideways on the bed so he could keep holding me down, he rubbed his face down the soft, rounded skin of my belly, burying his face for a moment in the curls at the vee of my thighs.

I could feel my juices flowing, my pussy aching for him to touch it. But Auric continued to torture me, blowing hotly against my clit. I bucked my hips hard; for a second I made contact with his hot mouth, and I moaned. Auric moved away and slid back up my body, making me mewl.

I couldn't handle the torture anymore. I needed him desperately. I wanted to turn the tables, and I did. Remembering my increased power and knowing

I was highly charged after our lovemaking, I pushed a bit with my power and flipped our positions so that I was on top, holding him down. His eyes widened, then he smiled, such a breathtaking, loving sight that I let go of his hands to cup his face and kiss him. His hands gripped my waist, lifting me and sliding me back 'til I perched above his cock, the swollen head nudging my wet lips. I sat down hard on his shaft, impaling myself on his length. He sucked in a breath, and his fingers dug into my waist. I leaned up into a sitting position and splayed my hands on his chest, swinging my hair back. I looked at him, lying there flushed, his body straining, but I wanted to see another face. I wanted to see the face he wore when he came.

I rode him like a cowgirl rides her horse—and her man—bouncing my bottom up and down on his cock, each thrust pushing him deeper inside me. And each time I rammed him in, his breathing came a little faster, his movements a little less controlled. I increased my pace, leaning forward to dangle my tits in his face, moaning myself when he flicked his tongue out against my nipples. This new position put a sweet friction on my clit that made me shiver in delight. My pelvic muscles quivered, squeezing his cock tighter and tighter. I moved back up to a sitting position again, panting just as quickly as he was. My rhythm became almost frantic, but I kept my eyes open. When he shouted my name and came deep inside me, I saw his face. He opened his eyes, the green of them blazing, the love in them so fierce, so strong I screamed and my body shattered into a million blazing pieces. My heart joined me in exploding with joy, and I thought I would die from the pleasure.

Slowly, I came back down to earth. My body cradled into his, his face nuzzled into my hair. And with my lover, my angel Auric, I fell asleep smiling.

I was no longer alone. I'd found love.

CHAPTER SIXTEEN

"WHAT'S YOUR FAVORITE DOUGHNUT?" AURIC asked as he nibbled on my neck.

"French crueler. Why are you asking? Don't tell me you make doughnuts, too?" I rolled over with a smile to see him propped on one elbow in my bed, looking deliciously rumpled. And naked. Utterly, deliciously, hickey-marked naked.

Sigh.

"No, I don't make doughnuts, but the coffee shop across the street does. I'll pop over for a second and grab us something. If any demons show up, save some for me, will you?"

I smiled at his comment. Protective of me didn't mean he didn't respect my ass-kicking abilities. Of course, being at my place, we had nothing to worry about. No demons allowed. Which was good because I had plans for my angel lover. Nefarious ones that involved more biting and pleasure. After my donut.

Auric hopped out of bed, his firm buttocks rippling as he located his scattered clothing. I rolled onto my tummy and watched him, feeling a different kind of hunger altogether.

"Let's skip breakfast and go right to fun." My smile deepened to see his cock already semi-hard.

His grin, on the other hand, was rueful. "If I wasn't afraid we'd pass out from hunger, I would. Don't worry, though. I have plans for you after breakfast."

That sounded promising. I let him finish dressing, giggling as he tried to stuff his hard shaft into his pants. He finally managed it by leaving the room because, apparently, I was too distracting.

I heard the door to the apartment close, and I sat up, stretching my naked body. My naked, sated body.

I suddenly realized something—I wasn't a virgin anymore! My dad would now have to find something new to harp about. Not only that, I could now brag about my exploits to my sisters.

Another big thrill and bonus? The strength I could feel coursing through me. Batteries were fully charged. I felt as if I could take on the world, which meant I'd have to be careful until I learned the boundaries of my increased power.

While Auric fetched us breakfast, I used the bathroom because even a supernatural like me needed to pee and brush her teeth.

Wandering naked out into my living room, I basked in the warm sunlight coming through the window. What a beautiful day.

I walked over to the window that looked down on the street. Auric had been gone only a moment, and I missed him already. I saw the coffee shop across the way and leaned on my elbows, watching for my lover—giggle—my stud—totally—my Auric, to saunter out.

As if thinking conjured him, the shop door opened and he walked out, a coffee tray in one hand, a bag in the other. I pressed my bare boobs up against the window, hoping he'd look up and see them.

When he'd reached the halfway mark in the street, I saw a shimmer as a portal materialized.

What the fuck?

A half-dozen largish demons—using cloaking magic so that to a normal human the spot they were in appeared as just a haze in the air—stepped out to form a ring around Auric. I immediately recognized the distinctive marks of Azazel, and my heart stuttered to a stop. I pounded on the window and screamed in rage as the demons dove on Auric and the coffee splashed to the ground. Too many fists pummeled. My lover vainly tried to defend himself, but his sword was still by the bed. He'd foolishly forgotten it in his quick jaunt across the street.

What a fatal error. Overcome, he could do nothing as they pulled his arms behind his back. As a compliment to his prowess, they also threw a noose, the metal links glinting in the sunlight, around his neck. The leash end was held by Azazel, a soon-to-be-very-sorry demon.

Azazel yanked on the leash, choking my beloved; Auric fell to his knees, and they bound his arms in matching silver cuffs.

His tortured face looked up at the window, bruises already mottling his features. I knew he saw me there. His lips moved, and I recognized the words "I love you" and something else, which I would have bet anything on was something along the lines of "Don't you dare save me." Like I'd listen.

Azazel noticed Auric ignoring him. The bastard demon glanced up at the window where I watched. He sneered and waved before he shoved Auric through the interdimensional rip, leaving me alone with my rage. I also felt something I'd never experienced before—utter fear for another person.

A part of me understood Auric's capture was a ploy to get to me. Well, I intended to reward them with what they wanted because I'd bet they didn't know about my new kick-ass powers. But they would really soon, and I'd make them sorry they'd ever disturbed a hair on Auric's head.

New dilemma, though. I needed to get to Hell, and unlike most demons, being part human—albeit a not-so-ordinary one—I couldn't just open a portal there. I'd need a demon to bring me over.

I scrounged for some clothes appropriate for the pit and threw them on the bed before digging out the phone that connected directly to Hades and my dad.

Phone hugged between my chin and shoulder, I hopped into a pair of black briefs.

After a few rings, a recording came on. "Sorry, but all the lines to Hell are currently busy. Your call is unfortunately not important to us, and we will not be keeping you in a queue. Call back again at your own peril." Cackling, maniacal laughter sounded, followed by a click.

I pulled the phone away from my ear and frowned at it. That had never happened before. If I couldn't get in touch with my dad, then how would I get to the pit and save my love?

While I finished dressing, I made a mental list of beings I knew who could open a portal. Bambi made the top of my list, and being my closest sister, I figured her for my best bet.

I dialed her number, and the phone rang and rang; I almost hung up before her voicemail picked up. The recording sounded rushed. "Gone back home to deal with some trouble. Hope I'll make it back. And little lamb, if this is you, do not, I repeat, do not follow."

The message did not have a beep at the end and, instead, hung up on me. Suddenly afraid, but needing to be sure, I called all the minions and relatives of Hell I knew in the area. One after another their phones either didn't answer or I got strange messages implying trouble back home.

What was going on? Had the coup my father scoffed at actually managed to cause some damage? Was my dad in danger? Even suckier, everybody else seemed to have been called back to Hell to fight; everyone, that was, except me.

No fair. I could kick ass with the best of them. I resented the fact that my possible mortality made them think I couldn't help. That they just expected me to stay home while everybody else did their part.

And what about Auric? He needed me, too. In fact, I wondered if perhaps his kidnapping might be tied into the whole situation going on back home in the pit.

I needed to find out more, but I'd run out of people to call. If only I had the power to open a portal myself.

I sat down on my couch, utterly dejected. And to think I'd dressed in my combat best: skin-tight black leggings, a black sleeveless tee that hugged my torso, and black running shoes—all fire retardant, of course.

I wanted to cry, but that wouldn't help Auric. I needed to keep my wits about me. There had to be something or someone I'd missed that could get me to Hades. Determined to go through my phone book again, I hopped up from the couch and happened to notice the crack I'd made in the wall when I'd shoved Auric into it by accident the previous day with my newfound power.

In retrospect, I felt kind of bad about that. Although, at the time, I hadn't known about my new super-duper powers.

I smacked myself in the forehead. Ow! Rubbing my sore head, I mused.

Maybe I didn't need anyone to open a portal for me. The problem before had always been power-related. I now had power, lots of it. I could feel it coursing under my skin.

Why not use it? I'd seen portals opened my entire life. Surely I could imitate.

I now had a plan. But before I descended into the depths of Hell, I needed to arm myself. Opening my toy cabinet, I armed myself to the teeth. Daggers hidden in sheaths all over my body, a pistol with heavy-duty tranquilizers at my waist—*if you can't kill 'em, put 'em to sleep, I say*—my unicorn hair whip, and the pièce de résistance—a gift from my father—my Hell sword. Forged of red steel and sharper than any mortal blade, my wicked sword had been specially crafted to slay demons; and as I slid it in the sheath I wore down the middle of my back, I made a promise to the blade—"You will taste demon blood today."

Ready to kick some ass, I went back to the living room, cleared a space in the center of the room, and sat down lotus style. Taking deep breaths, I cleared my mind, mentally preparing myself to open the portal.

I traced a rectangle in the air and repeated the words I'd heard hundreds of times, half-expecting to fail like I had in the past when I'd tried. As soon as the last word left my lips, the power in my body began to drain, supporting the glowing portal that formed itself in front of me. I gaped at the dimensional doorway. I might have done that for a while had the fierce siphoning of my magic to keep it open not moved me forward. I needed to get to the other side and close the door before I depleted my magical reserves too far.

I jumped to my feet and gave my hair a shake while wishing I had time to check my lip-gloss. But time was pressing so I strode through, head held high —after all, I was Lucifer's daughter and one of the heirs to the Kingdom of Hell. This was my world. And I was coming to take it back.

CHAPTER SEVENTEEN

I EMERGED FROM THE PORTAL TO SILENCE. Complete, eerie, utter stillness.

I let the rift collapse and then looked around. The barren landscape around me with the shells of once-tall buildings, red rock, and ruin looked like Hades, but where were the damned? The demons? The noise?

Hell was not a quiet place. There was only a semblance of night and day here, along with an eternity of suffering—lots of suffering. Well, for the truly evil and misbehaved that was. The rest, which made up the majority, who just didn't seem able to achieve Heaven's lofty standard, just worked and lived here, millions upon millions of them.

I walked the silent streets, apprehension and wariness my only companions.

What had happened? Where had everyone gone?

I figured if there was one place that would have life—or death, depending on how you looked at it—it would be the palace. My dad's home in Hell and where I'd spent most of my childhood.

Quickly, I walked through the outer town that bordered my father's estate, my black boots quickly becoming coated with the fine ash that sifted constantly from the sky.

Reaching the gates that surround my father's compound, I stopped, mystified again because the gates were closed. I hadn't even known they could do that. In all my years, those giant rusted monstrosities gaped open. A dare to those who might think to attack.

No one ever did.

However, with them now shut, that had to mean someone was inside, right? I pounded on the towering rusted doors.

The sound echoed, unnaturally loud in the barren stillness. I had to fight an urge to hide, for surely that noise would bring someone running, and they might not be the good—er, bad—guys.

Silence prevailed, and the gate stayed shut.

I began to wonder if I'd messed up the portal

somehow. This couldn't be Hell. I must have made an error. Perhaps, if I went to my apartment and tried again... I sketched a portal in the space in front of me.

Nothing.

I tried again, concentrating hard on my living room and pulling on my power. And again, nothing happened.

Really freaked now, I began walking away from the palace, looking for something, anything, that would end this deafening silence.

My feet tripped over the debris in the streets. I fell to my knees in the powdery dust, my hands hitting the ground hard, and I cried out. As I knelt there on my hands and knees, cursing my clumsiness and uneasiness—me afraid? Never!—I thought I heard an echo of sound. A voice.

My head shot up, and I sniffed the air much as a dog would, but my senses were dulled by the sifting ash. Without even thinking, I pulled on a little of my power to enhance my senses and inhaled deeply. I was rewarded with a familiar scent.

Auric!

Jumping to my feet, I ran, suddenly as nimble as a deer in flight. I leapt over the obstacles in my path, heading to my angel. I could already taste my revenge. It would be sweet—and deadly.

As I jogged, I began to recognize the road I trod on, and I slowed my feet. I didn't need to dash head-long and announce my presence. I knew where they held Auric, the most sacred place in the pit. A place that frightened many, but offered solace to others, where the nine circles of Hell converged—the abyss.

Created a long time ago due to the overcrowding in Hades, the abyss was a person's final destination. After you'd done your penance for your misdeeds in life—which tended to be short, for most people—the damned were given a choice; live and work in Hell, or end it all in the abyss.

My dad called it a 'people recycler'. People went in, and everything that made them who they were got wiped, and their energy, called souls by most, emerged to live again—reincarnation made real.

Now, you would think that once people got to Hell, most would choose this route. Why live here, you ask? Odd as it seemed, people having died once tended to be more frightened the second time, especially knowing that everything they knew, everything they were, would disappear. A lot of the damned preferred to eke out an existence in the pit, surrounded by friends and family, rather than spin the wheel of chance and end up a nobody in a new body and who-knew-what kind of life.

It drove my dad nuts that more people didn't jump in, but he never forced anyone unless they disrupted the natural flow of Hell, which, in turn, disrupted my father's pursuit of pleasure—AKA chasing women. When that happened, the offender was rapidly dropped, usually kicking and screaming, into the abyss, and life, of a sort, went on.

Eventually, most people did move on. It took a few hundred years sometimes, but by themselves, or sometimes as a pair, and even a few times a whole family, would take the plunge, swearing to find each other again in their new lives. And for all we knew, they did.

Bringing my mind back to the task at hand, though, I worried about the choice of location. I didn't know what would happen if Auric—not quite human, no longer an angel—got tossed into the abyss. Would the abyss be able to make him live again, or would it hold on to this unknown factor, unable to rebirth him but also unable to set him free?

I would make sure nothing happened. My plan was to ensure Auric survived, at all cost.

Quietly approaching the area where the nine

circles converged, I pulled out my Hell sword with only the slightest whisper of sound. I crept through the rocky outcropping, emerging onto the stone-strewn ring of dirt that circled the gaping chasm that was the abyss.

Kneeling at the edge, arms still bound, head bowed, was Auric.

He's alive! Exultation made me want to rush forward and touch him, but if we were both to survive, I needed to keep my wits and follow the training I'd painstakingly gone through. The years and years of instruction by my father and my teachers had taught me one primary lesson —survival.

I walked with silent steps toward Auric. I didn't trust this unnatural stillness or this lack of enemy in sight. I didn't need the prickle of awareness between my shoulder blades to know someone, or something, watched.

My eyes flicked left and right, searching for motion. I knew Azazel had to be here somewhere. A small pebble rolled, a miniscule sound, and yet Auric's face lifted, and with one good eye—the other being swollen shut—he looked straight at me, his expression utterly stricken.

"Muriel, no," he croaked. "Go back. It's a trap."

Just like a man to state the obvious. "I know." I smiled with what I hoped was reassurance while inwardly seething. I could tell he'd put up a valiant fight. His body bled from multiple wounds, and the thick chains that bound him told of his strength, a strength they feared. I wanted to scream at those who'd hurt him then rip their innards out and watch them as they died.

Bloodthirsty? Damned right. They'd hurt my love. Being my father's daughter, I would make them pay.

And I will enjoy it.

From above, I heard the beating of leathery wings and down floated Azazel, a cold smile on his demonic face. As if his presence were the signal, other demons crept out of hiding, cutting off my retreat to the rear and penning me in on the sides.

Triumph glittered in Azazel's eyes. "About time you showed up, Satan's whelp. I was beginning to wonder if we needed to send you pictures of your boyfriend to get you to come."

"I'm here now. Let him go." I didn't figure the traitor would, but I had to try.

"Satana, Satana, Satana." Azazel spoke to me, shaking his head and finger at me like a naughty child. "Do you really think I'm going to do that? My master is quite interested in this angel. He has plans for him. Painful plans."

"Make new ones. You can't have him."

"Can't?" Azazel laughed. "We already do. And there's nothing you can do to change that, unless..." He tapered off slyly.

"What do you want?"

I heard Auric moan, "No, Mur—" A plea that was cut off when Azazel turned and kicked Auric, hard, in the ribs. My angel didn't cry out, although I knew he had to be hurting. And that was just one more reason why Azazel would die. Very painfully.

Forcing my gaze away from Auric, I concentrated on Azazel and asked again, my voice flecked with ice, "What do you want?"

"My master wants you, willing and docile, in exchange for the life of the angel."

No real surprise. Everyone wanted me. In this case, I could easily surmise that they planned to kill me, but they'd make me hurt first.

I understood that, but even more, I refused to allow Auric to die for me. I loved him. I would take this pain from him. I would die for him.

"Let us hammer out the terms first." I knew

better than to just give in without negotiation. My father was the king of loopholes when it came to promises, and I'd learned well. "I will give myself to your *master*"—my lip curled in disdain—"willingly in exchange for Auric, on the condition that he is transported, with no further harm, to inside my bar. I will not fight your master, so long as Auric lives and is safe." It was the best I could do, for Auric and myself.

Being a douchebag, Azazel pretended to think about it. I took that moment to glance briefly at Auric and saw him shaking his head, his lips mouthing, "No."

I looked away, lest I begin to cry.

"I accept the deal." Azazel grinned, his pointed teeth prominent and his eyes black, bottomless orbs. "Shall we shake on it, Satan's spawn?"

I spat in my hand and held it out to seal the deal, a little zing of power acknowledging it and binding Azazel to its terms. This interesting aspect of deal-making with demons had been created long ago by an ancient power whose origins no one remembered. It ensured the demons held to the pacts they made.

Personally, I didn't care how it worked so long as I could use it to my advantage to save Auric.

Knowing I had little time, I walked toward Auric.

"Where do you think you are going, Satana?" hissed Azazel.

"To say goodbye. Surely you wouldn't begrudge me that," I snapped. "You've got your precious deal. Let me kiss him one last time before you send him back, and I will go to your master willingly."

I resumed my walk, Auric's injuries looking even worse up close. Tears pooled in my eyes, and I couldn't stop them from falling as I fell to my knees in front of him.

"Why?" he asked, his voice cracking. "I would have died for you."

"I know," I said softly, reaching out to touch his cheek. "Allow me to do the same. I love you." I leaned forward and kissed his lips one last time. The salt of tears and blood flavored them, and even with everything going on around us, I felt a spurt of energy enter me at this final, intimate touch.

"Goodbye, Auric. Remember me," I whispered before standing up and taking a step back.

Auric threw his head back and howled. The misery in that sound made my throat tighten painfully. I hoped he'd eventually forgive me for this decision and forget me.

"No. I won't let you do this!" Auric began to struggle, his thick muscles straining as he thrashed in his chains. My eyes widened when I heard the squealing sound of the metal twisting. However, his berserker rage was not enough to break the ties that bound him.

Two demons rushed forward at Azazel's signal and grabbed Auric around the upper arms. Auric refused to give up, and he twisted and cried out hoarsely. Azazel called a portal, and his minions hauled Auric through.

I'd done it. Auric was safe.

With a triumphant grin, Azazel beckoned me.

As if I'd scurry to his side like an obedient bitch. I turned a cold stare on him. "When your demons get back, show me that he is safe; and then I will go to your master."

Azazel growled in frustration, but I just smiled at him evilly as I fingered the hilt of my sword. Within a few minutes, the two demons returned, and Azazel sketched a hexagonal pattern in the air. He shouted a few coarse-sounding words, the air in front of me blurred with colors, and when they came into focus...

I could see the inside of my bar. Bambi, David, Percy, Christopher, and a host of other familiar faces crowded around Auric's slumped form on the floor. While I couldn't hear, I could watch as Percy heaved Auric to his feet and help him stagger to the bar.

Auric's lips moved, as he no doubt recounted what had happened. My heart tore at the grim and sad expression on his face.

The image wavered and disappeared.

"Happy now?" snarled Azazel. "Now come and kneel before me."

A wide grin stretched my lips and I really enjoyed saying, "No."

My refusal took him aback. "We made a deal, Satana. You cannot renege."

"I'm not reneging. I remember quite clearly saying I would give myself to your master and not fight your master. I never said anything about you and your master's minions."

I quite enjoyed the look of consternation on his face, quickly followed by rage.

"Bitch!"

"Is that the best you can come up with, you slimy, lizard-ball-licking, puny-dicked excuse for a demon?" At his cry of rage, I laughed even as I pulled my Hell sword out of its sheath, the rippling fires of Hades gleaming along its blade, matching the fires that I knew shone from my eyes.

Baring my teeth ferally, I stalked forward. "Now you will pay for your sins, Azazel."

But he ever was a coward.

"Take her," he screamed, and suddenly I found myself surrounded by demons.

Game on.

This was what I'd trained for. This was what my rage needed.

I hacked and slashed with my sword, my technique perhaps not as fluid as Auric's, but it did the job. Limbs separated, demons screamed, and blood gushed; and all the while, I laughed hysterically.

Deep down inside, I knew I couldn't win, and I didn't care if I died. I'd saved Auric. That was all that mattered. But before I gasped my last breath, I'd make sure I took a shitload of the treacherous bastards with me. These demons had betrayed my father and hurt my lover.

Revenge was my middle name. Okay, not really, but I totally wanted to get it legally changed.

Amidst the cacophony of battle, I could hear Azazel shouting, but I ignored him. I put all my focus into fighting instead. The magic in my body gave me strength and agility like I'd never experienced before. I twirled and danced among the horde that surrounded me. Every slice of the blade scored a deadly wound. I found the rhythm for my dance of death in the screams and cries of the wounded and dying.

"I am Satana Muriel Baphomet," I screamed. "Princess of Hell. I am your judge, jury, and executioner. And you will all die!"

And they did. Some silently. Some wailing. All of them spilled blood, a fluid the hungry soil absorbed. I swung and swung and...

Suddenly I staggered as I jabbed my sword and hit nothing. Surely I hadn't killed them all.

It took me but a moment to realign my focus and view the world around me, a place now strewn with limbs and bodies and retreating demons. The scent of blood and gore hung heavy and nauseating around me. I felt the wetness on my skin, skin covered in the slime of death, and wondered if my savage appearance was why the demons who were left backed away looking fearful.

Scary as I surely appeared, I doubted I was the reason for their trepidation.

Taking a deep breath, I turned around.

My sword fell from my numb fingers, as the promise I'd made took hold of my body and will, forcing me to obey.

I fell to my knees as Azazel's master approached.

"Who are you?" I asked. I tried to see within the shadowy cowl that masked the would-be usurper.

The voice, when it came, surprised me. Light

and almost musical in tone, I couldn't decide if it belonged to a male or female—or maybe even an 'other'.

"Bastard daughter of Satan, long have I watched thee. I had almost wondered if perhaps thou had escaped the curse of thy father's blood. But I smell the stink of man upon you. Unwed slut, you art no better than thy mother. It pains me to think I must touch thy flesh, unpure as it is, but thou hast something I need."

"Show your face, coward. Why do you hide?"

Chiming laughter, musical like bells, rang forth from the hood, yet the sweet sound gave me chills. Such dulcet notes should not belong to the wrongness I sensed emanating from this being.

"I will reveal myself when the time is right. A pity thou shall not live to see my grand victory. Goodbye, daughter of Lucifer."

I wanted to fight. My body strained at the invisible bonds of the pact I'd made, but they bound me tightly to my word. Azazel's master approached, and I could only stare into the dark recesses of its cowl, trying to see its face.

Failing. I perceived nothing but shadows.

The figure reached out a slender, pale hand, the

skin translucent and unblemished. It pressed its seemingly innocuous palm to my forehead.

Unlike the battle, where I'd laughed off my pain and injuries, this time I screamed.

CHAPTER EIGHTEEN

ONCE THE PAIN STARTED, I THOUGHT IT WOULD never end. Crushing and debilitating agony consumed me. It wasn't long before I began praying for death, anything to escape the unbearable torture.

I couldn't tell how long I screamed, but eventually I did finally stop and found myself lying on the ground twitching uncontrollably, as if caught in a grand mal seizure. I was unfortunately still aware, inside my prison of pain—barely—and sharing this awareness with me was that parasitic monster Azazel called master. Like a leech, this monstrous being sucked at my power, and it didn't simply drain it from me, oh no. It savagely ripped the force from me, leaving me feeling weaker and weaker.

Through my head flashed memories, so fast I

couldn't see them, as the being sifted through my mind as if searching for something. Back, back in time, Azazel's master looked until it found the day I came to live with my father, Satan.

I sensed the monster's excitement as it halted its mind-rape and slowly moved my memories back a day. The day my life changed forever. It eagerly attempted to access those memories that even I could not remember, and suddenly shields slammed down in my head and a powerful voice screamed, "Be gone." A flash of bright light followed, and I found myself flying weightlessly through the air before crashing to the ground.

Ow. I shook my head dazedly. What had just happened? Did I care? At least that monster no longer touched me. Yet, I wasn't safe.

I lay with my face and arm hanging over the edge of the abyss. My body throbbed painfully, covered in bruises and cuts, while my head ached horribly. I could hear voices through the ringing in my ears. With great effort, I turned my face, and I opened one bleary eye to see the robed figure pick itself up off the ground.

As it came striding toward me angrily, Azazel at its heels, I'm ashamed to say I whimpered.

I looked longingly at the abyss. Just a little effort, and all my pain would be gone. Or so I hoped. I couldn't be sure the abyss wouldn't hurt just as badly, but right now, caught between certain pain and death and possible pain and death, I knew which I chose.

From above, I heard the beating of wings and cries from all sides. Ignoring them all, I drew on my last reserves of strength and rolled my body into the chasm, and hopefully oblivion.

I heard a familiar voice bellow, "No!"

It had sounded like Auric, an impossibility I knew, and probably a product of a hallucinating mind. Auric was half dead, but safe in my bar. I'd saved him. It had to be a trick.

Too late anyway. I'd fallen into the abyss, and my limp body tumbled down weightlessly.

Then my descent abruptly stopped.

Powerful arms gripped me, and I heard the ponderous sound of wings beating. I opened my eyes, and through a haze, I thought I saw Auric, his visage fierce and angry. His lips were drawn tight, and his green eyes blazed with fury. If I hadn't hurt so much, I would have smiled; he looked so handsome. Sprouting from his back, I caught the impression of dark wings.

"Auric," I murmured weakly, "you got your wings back."

And then the pain became too much again, and I passed out.

CHAPTER NINETEEN

I woke, snuggled in a pair of familiar arms, cradled protectively. I was glad for their strength because I felt so weak.

However, nice as they were, memories began crowding my mind. Reality intruded as I remembered falling and being caught. Had Auric joined me in the abyss? Had he joined me in the ultimate death?

But wait, that couldn't be. The abyss wiped a person clean. I still knew who I was—the most awesome princess of Hell. Thinking harder, I recalled an impression of wings at Auric's back. Was he an angel again?

I wanted to open my eyes and ask him, but I realized we weren't alone. I smelled brimstone and heard people murmuring. Were we both prisoners, still in Hades? Had the master captured us and kept us for a nefarious purpose?

I trembled, overwhelming fear of the pain still too fresh a memory. The arms around me tightened, cocooning, and reassuring me without words that I was safe now.

I felt another measure of relief when I heard my father's roaring voice. "What do you mean she's still unconscious?"

If my dad was yelling, then it meant, against all odds, we were safe. I lived and was with Auric again. But how?

The chest against my cheek rumbled. "Would you stop yelling? She's going to be all right. The healer says most of her wounds are superficial, and look: most of them have healed already."

My father spoke more quietly. "It's not her body I'm worried about. That thing did something to her mind."

"I know, but Muriel's strong," said Auric with firm assurance. "I've never known a braver, stronger person. She'll be all right. She has to be." It sounded like Auric wanted to convince himself along with my father.

It was past time I let them know I'd survived—albeit barely. I forced an eyelid open and croaked, "Water."

Immediately, concerned green eyes peered into mine. "You're back." Auric kissed my forehead lightly, and I felt a little stronger.

"What's that? My girl's awake. Muriel, talk to me," said my father. His anxious face shoved Auric's aside, and his burning eyes gazed upon me with concern.

"Hi, Daddy," I whispered.

"Damn fool girl, what were you thinking, going in there by yourself? You and your boyfriend here are a well-matched pair of idiots."

Auric shifted me to a sitting position on his lap, and a glass of water was thrust into my hands. I gulped it eagerly, washing away the dust from Hell and feeling a lot better in the process.

I finally took note of our surroundings and realized we were all in my bar. A ring of familiar faces stood around, their clothing and skin smudged with the ash of Hell. Just what had happened after I passed out?

"Um, anyone want to explain what happened after I fainted?" I looked at Auric, his face once again whole—not a blemish to be seen. Impossible. Even with his ability to heal faster than mortals, he'd been so badly injured. "Auric?"

"Yes, well, after you foolishly traded yourself for me, I ended up back at the bar. Bambi had just come back from Hell and was looking for you when I arrived."

Bambi approached me, her face smeared with dirt and her clothes in rags. And of course, she still looked drop-dead gorgeous. I probably looked like a refugee from Hades—hey, wait, I was.

"As soon as I heard what happened to you, I went to get Dad," said Bambi, touching me lightly.

"Bloody damn nervy of them to take you like that," blustered my father. "When I got to the bar, your man here begged for help to go back and save you. Of course, he looked like shit, so initially I said no."

Auric rolled his eyes. "Actually, what you said was, 'Boy, right now you're more useless than a third fucking tit'."

I giggled. Yeah, that sounded like my father.

"Anyway, your man here asked me to help him save you. So I fixed him all up, even gave him some wings, and next thing you know, the damn fool goes off on his own to save you without waiting for anyone."

My eyes widened in horror. Auric had made a deal with my father. Oh, no. "Daddy how could you take advantage of his love for me like that? You give him back his soul, right now!" I had given myself to save Auric from death, and I wasn't about to let my father keep his soul for saving me.

My father frowned at me. "What are you talking about? I didn't take a thing from your boyfriend. I only healed him and gave him powers, on the condition he keep you alive. He did that, so we're even."

I think my jaw dropped. No way. My father had to have created some kind of loophole. I'd have to make sure to see the contract later.

"It's true," said Auric. "My soul is still yours, Muriel."

"Make me barf," grumbled her dad.

My lover ignored him. "Now that I have back all the powers I had as an angel, actually, more power, I think. I even have wings. Mind you, they're not white anymore. My new shadow wings are more of a charcoal gray, but I can live with that. It's better than living without you. It's also what helped me save you."

"Tell me everything." I wanted to know every detail.

With a few voices joining in, I heard about how Auric, as soon as he found himself healed, used his recovered magic to open a portal to Hell and come after me. My brave champion. He arrived in time to see me tumbling over the edge of the abyss. He swooped down and carried me out then stood over me, fighting with my Hell sword until the cavalry arrived.

"You should have seen him, Muriel," my father said, looking impressed. "Swinging your sword around like a Viking of old. Standing guard over your body and growling like a rabid dog at all who approached. Between the two of you, there was barely anything left to fight." My daddy didn't bother to hide his disappointment. "You could have left the rest of us a few to kill."

"I would have figured you'd had your fill of battle. What with everyone being called back to Hell to fight," I said, still miffed they hadn't thought to call me.

"That's just it," my father grumbled. "There was no fight. We'd received word that the coup was coming, so I called everyone home to fight, and we were waiting, ready..."

"Everyone except me," I muttered.

My father drew himself up indignantly. "You, my daughter, happened to be the first one I called, but no matter what I dialed, it went right to voicemail."

My resentment slipped away. "You really wanted me there?"

"Damn straight, I did. You're the best demon slayer I've got."

"Ah, Daddy." I totally choked up.

Satan cleared his throat. "Yes, well, there we were, ready to kick the mutineers where it hurt, when it hit."

"What?" I asked, leaning forward eagerly. "Trans-dimensional creature? Spirits from Purgatory? What attacked?"

"Nothing. Everyone kind of fell asleep. When we woke up and found no one to fight, I sent everyone home."

I laughed. I couldn't help it; my father looked so put out. "But how? A spell of that magnitude? It seems impossible."

"Whoever we're up against has access to some pretty potent ancient magic. I'll be talking to my scientists and wizards back in Hell to find out what happened. I may even call my brother. This doesn't smell like the kind of thing God would do, which means I'm pretty sure he'll want answers, too. We'll be better prepared next time."

I processed what my father said, and my body shivered lightly in fear. Next time? I didn't want to ever go through the agony of what that being had done to me. My mind still felt raw, and my body so weak. And what if they came after Auric again? "Do you mean to tell me that Azazel and his master are still loose?"

At my words, almost everyone dropped their heads and pretended to look elsewhere. Even my father cleared his throat and looked at his toes.

Auric was the one who answered me. "They escaped. Standing guard over you, I couldn't chase them when they saw the tide turning. They left, just as your father and reinforcements arrived."

"So they're still out there?" I said quietly while trying to push that little quiver of fear down. I used my trepidation to instead coax the fires of my rage.

Auric nodded. "They are, but don't worry; I'll protect you better next time."

"Me, too," chimed in my father.

I arched my brows. "Protect me? Fuck that.

When I find them"—and I would—"I'll expect you by my side ready to fight."

My father laughed out loud at my vehement words, and for a second, I worried that I might have freaked out Auric with my bloodthirstiness. But my angel was made of sterner stuff.

His face turned hard, and when he spoke, his tone sounded even harsher. "I intend to hurt them before I kill them. They will pay for what they did to you."

I shivered in his arms at his words. I wanted to feel sad that my love for him had already changed him, made him colder; but truth be told, I found this mercenary side of him exciting. So exciting I wanted to get him alone.

I faked a yawn.

"Muriel needs to rest," announced Auric with authority. He stood, cradling me in his arms. I saw my father whisper something in Auric's ear, and I frowned. I didn't like secrets.

But Auric smiled down at me, and I forgave them. Hey, at least my father was talking to him instead of trying to kill him.

From the comfort of arms that refused to let me go, I waved goodbye as Auric strode out of the bar.

"You can't carry me all the way home," I pointed out.

"Be quiet. I can and will. If I had my way, I'd never let you go again."

Auric called forth his new shadow wings. They were beautiful: charcoal-colored, with silky looking plumage. When he beat them, their massive breadth spread wide behind him. We left the ground and the bar behind.

Auric swooped through the air like an angel of the night, and I smiled up at him. "Are you sure my dad didn't make you promise anything stupid in exchange for them?"

"I wouldn't call promising to take care and protect you stupid. I'd planned on doing that anyway. He just gave me the tools I needed to do so. I meant what I sang to you." Auric sang to me softly again the words to the song, our song.

When he finished serenading me, I leaned my head on his chest. "I love you, Auric."

"My soul belongs to you, Muriel. I will not let you down again."

"You never did." It made my heart hurt to hear him say that. He'd done more for me than I'd ever expected from anyone. I'd never expected to find a love so great that I would be willing to die for it, let alone have that love returned in the same measure. I made a promise to myself—I would do everything I could to be worthy of Auric's love.

I kissed the edge of his jaw lightly, not wanting to inflame him until we'd landed but, at the same time, needing to touch him. Thankfully, we soon landed on a fire escape outside his building.

"Shouldn't we go to my place? It's demon-proof." Azazel and his master were still loose, and I wanted no interruptions with what I intended to do to Auric.

"Your dad had the place spelled. It's what he was whispering to me before we left. No one can get in at all, not even him. He said it was his gift to you, for"—and here Auric blushed—"for—um—finally losing your virginity."

I laughed as Auric opened the door and slid us into the vast space of his loft. I was still chortling when he deposited me on his gi-normous bed. But I stopped laughing and watched with interest when he stripped off his shirt.

"I know you probably want a shower and are hungry and tired, but I need to touch you. I need to feel you and know you're safe, with me."

"That's good because I need the same thing." I opened up my arms to him, and he fell on me, the weight of his body welcome.

His lips caressed mine tenderly, and his hands cupped my face. He paused to look at me, and I could have sworn I saw a shimmer in his eyes. "I almost died when I saw you plunge into the abyss. If I hadn't saved you, I would have followed you."

"Oh, Auric." I covered his face with kisses, reaffirming to him that I lived while reassuring myself of his wholeness.

Frantic with need, a need based on more than just lust, he stripped us both, and when we lay skin to skin, he entered me slowly, my sex already damp and ready for him. Gently, he claimed me, his hands cradling my face as his eyes bored into mine. I didn't close my eyes. I wanted to see him, to reassure myself this was no dream. We'd both survived. We could be together.

His pace increased, and I met him thrust for thrust, the blood pounding through my veins, power starting to build inside me, energizing me. Our bodies intricately joined, we rode the pleasure wave higher and higher. When we orgasmed, both gasping at the same time, I could swear I felt our souls touch. And, for one glorious moment, we were one.

When we came back to reality, I snuggled him, already feeling so much stronger.

He kissed my temple softly. "I love you, Muriel."

"I love you, too, but if you ever do something so dangerously stupid again, I will kill you myself." I leaned on an elbow to frown at him.

"I wasn't going to let you die," he repeated stubbornly.

"I wasn't just talking about that. I was talking about your deal with my father. You made a deal with the Devil."

Auric propped himself against the headboard and met me, glare for glare. "I would do anything to protect you. So get over it."

"Get over it?" I almost gasped. "Because of your deal, now you'll never go back to Heaven. You're damned now, Auric."

Auric lay back on the bed, hands laced behind his head, a huge smile on his face. "Yes, yes, I am. So stop your bitching and get back to sinning with me. Or," he said with a promising glint, "I might just have to put you over my knee and punish you for putting yourself in danger and disobeying me in the first place."

Oh my. I'd truly corrupted him. How wickedly lovely.

I didn't let him spank me—that night—although I did torture him quite a bit with my tongue until he screamed for mercy. After all, no one told me what I could or couldn't do. Then he tortured me back, in such delicious ways that I promised to obey him. Of course, I lied. I did have a reputation to maintain.

When all was said and done, our mutual punishment lasted two glorious days. The lesson I learned? I needed to be bad more often.

EPILOGUE

A week later…

"I don't see why we have to do this," grumbled Auric as he set the table.

"He's my father. If we're going to be together, you're going to have to get used to him." Said for the umpteenth time as I pulled off the lids of the Chinese food I'd ordered.

"I agree with the angel," said my father's voice as he suddenly appeared.

"Daddy!" I ran over to hug him.

"I thought you told me this place was demon-proof?" Auric frowned at my dad.

"I lied." My father grinned, completely unabashed.

I hid a smirk behind a hand. It was nice to know some things never changed.

"What's this all about, Muriel?" asked my daddy, intentionally sitting down at the head of the table.

"What, can't a girl have dinner with her two favorite guys?" At their sour looks, I sighed. "Listen. I love both of you, and I can't stand it that you guys can't even be civil to each other."

"He's the Devil," muttered Auric.

"You're sleeping with my daughter." My father retorted with an evil glare.

"Enough," I shouted.

Daddy and my angel looked at me with hurt expressions. I crossed my arms and angled my chin. "I really don't care if you don't like each other. However, you will be civil to one another, or I will take action."

Auric grimaced and, with a pained voice, said, "I'll make an effort if he does."

"Why does everyone always blame me?" ranted my father.

"Because you're Satan!" sputtered Auric.

My father laughed. "Boy, you are way too easy to get going."

Auric opened his mouth and shut it. Then

opened it again. "You mean you're doing it on purpose to rile me up?"

"Of course I am." My father grinned devilishly, an expression he'd coined after too much infernal grog one night.

"So you mean, when you told me you were going to string me up by my intestines over the abyss while letting crows peck at my eyes for corrupting your daughter, that was a joke?"

My father slapped his knee and guffawed.

I bit my lip, but the giggle came out anyway. "Dad, you didn't?"

"I said it, but I don't intend to do it. Much as it pains me, I can see my girl loves you and you love her back. Why do you think I allowed you to be with her?"

"What do you mean allowed?" I exclaimed, closely echoed by Auric.

"Oh, please." My father snorted. "You're my daughter, Muriel. If I didn't think Auric would care for you as much as I did, I'd have had him killed after your first meeting."

"Oh, Daddy." I tossed down my napkin as I got up so I could throw my arms around his neck. "That's the most beautiful thing you've ever said to me. I love you, too."

My father patted me awkwardly on my back. "Um. Yeah. Whatever."

When I sat back down, dabbing at the tears in my eyes, I saw Auric looking at my father and me, shaking his head, but a ghost of a smile hovered on his lips.

Daddy grinned at him. "Welcome to the family, *son*."

Auric blanched for just a second before recovering and, with a smile that spelled payback, said, "Well, I'm glad you feel that way, sir, since Muriel and I have decided to move in together."

My father razzed Auric for a bit about this, but I could tell he did it out of habit. Even more importantly, he'd accepted Auric as my boyfriend, and when my daddy left later on, he hugged me and whispered, "I'm so proud of you, Muriel, living in sin." I think he might have even choked up a bit. For my part, I was glad I'd finally done something Dad approved of.

And even happier, I'd found love.

* * *

IN ANOTHER DIMENSION, hidden from Heaven and Hell, someone watched the cozy dinner via a scrying mirror. At its conclusion, the heavily cloaked figure paced the cave it called home, musing on what it had learned. The plan to capture Satana and the secrets she hid within her mind had failed, although the power it had drained...

Mmm, delicious.

The addition of the fallen angel to the mix had proven to be an unexpected wrinkle. But perhaps this would work to its advantage. Muriel's powers kept growing. She'd make a formidable weapon in the right hands, especially with the right leverage. Perhaps it was time to deviate from the original plan and timeline. Time to put in motion something more daring. Something that would make both Heaven and Hell take notice.

And if that failed, there was always next time.

Find out what happens next : <u>Snowballs in Hell</u>.

CPSIA information can be obtained
at www.ICGtesting.com
Printed in the USA
LVHW031534230920
666818LV00004B/242

9 781773 840116